GW01459799

Guy de Maupassant

The Rondoli Sisters
and Other Selected Short Stories

Translated with an introduction and notes by
Michael Jones

Pen Press

© Michael Jones 2011

All rights reserved

No part of this publication may be reproduced, stored in a retrieval system, or transmitted in any form or by any means, without the prior permission in writing of the publisher, nor be otherwise circulated in any form of binding or cover other than that in which it is published and without a similar condition including this condition being imposed on the subsequent purchaser.

First published in Great Britain

All paper used in the printing of this book has been made from wood grown in managed, sustainable forests.

ISBN13: 978-1-78003-237-5

Printed and bound in the UK
Pen Press is an imprint of
Indepenpress Publishing Limited
25 Eastern Place
Brighton
BN2 1GJ

A catalogue record of this book is available from
the British Library

Cover design by Jacqueline Abromeit

Contents

INTRODUCTION

Guy de Maupassant was born in the chateau de Miromesnil near Dieppe in 1850. His mother Laure de Poittevin came from a family of wealthy manufacturers who lived near Fécamp and had a holiday house at Etretat. Little is known about his father Gustave de Maupassant except that he came from Lorraine, was easy going, worked in a bank in Paris and was separated from his wife. However he did contribute to his son's education and upkeep.

Maupassant received a good education, first, locally at Yvetot, then at Rouen and finally in Paris where he studied law. His career as a writer may have been encouraged by the fact that his mother, Laure, was friendly with the poet Bouilhet and the novelist Flaubert.

When the Franco-Prussian war broke out in 1870 Maupassant was drafted into an administrative department of the French army and was based both at Rouen and Le Havre. He witnessed the German entry into Paris and was lucky not to have been taken prisoner. When Peace was restored in 1871 Maupassant first obtained unpaid employment in the Ministry of the Marine and then a permanent post as a clerk. He settled in Paris and spent his free time rowing on the Seine at Argenteuil and consorting with young women many of whom undoubtedly were prostitutes. Not surprisingly in 1877 he was diagnosed with syphilis. On the other hand thanks to an introduction from Flaubert he cultivated his connections in Parisian literary circles and met up with Zola, Daudet and Turgenev amongst others. He started writing some short stories and small volumes of verse. One of his poems 'Une Fille' was published in a literary review and he was prosecuted for an offence against morality but fortunately the case was dropped.

In 1880 Maupassant published his short story about an incident in the Franco-Prussian war – 'Boule de Suif.' This was hailed as a masterpiece and was an immediate success. Consequently Maupassant resigned from his job at the Ministry and decided to devote his life to a career as a professional writer.

For the next dozen years Maupassant's literary output was amazing – 300 short stories, six full length novels, verse, plays and articles on topical subjects for the newspapers. Maupassant also did a lot of travelling and published several volumes of his accounts of his voyages. The Côte d'Azur, Italy, Corsica and North Africa were his favourite destinations and in 1885 he spent a few days in England at the invitation of Lord Rothschild. At the time Maupassant was also much feted by high society in Paris but although some of his stories show traces of snobbery as regards people in other parts of France, he never lost contact with the country folk he knew in Normandy where he passed his childhood and where he spent his holidays. Much of his writing reflects the character of the people and their pastimes there.

Although most of his short stories were initially published in newspapers, Maupassant made a great deal of money from the publishers of the collections and from his novels and he was much sought after by editors. So much so that in 1889 he was able to purchase a second much larger yacht called 'Bel-Ami' which he based both at Cannes and Antibes with a professional crew. (Both Maupassant's yachts were named 'Bel-Ami' which was the title of one of his most successful novels). In 1887 Maupassant wrote an account of a flight he had made in a balloon called 'Le Horla' which incidentally was the title of one of his more 'fantastic' stories.

At the end of 1891 Maupassant's disease finally caught up with him and after an unsuccessful attempt at suicide he was committed to an asylum near Paris where he died in 1893 at the age of 43.

Such are the very brief facts of Maupassant's crowded, short and exciting life. As for the selection of his stories printed in this book many are obviously autobiographical or related from the experiences of his friends. French critics have described most of them with adjectives such as '*leste*', '*grivois*' and '*boulevard-ier*', words which are almost impossible to translate into English. Their equivalents would probably be 'light weight', 'flippant', the type of gossip that could be picked up in the street or in the pub and certainly not the sort of tales that one would read to one's grandchildren. But of course they are much more than that and they are never pornographic. Maupassant with uncanny accuracy deals with all the relationships between sexes: love, prostitution, seduction, marriage, divorce and adultery; even paternity (another subject which fascinated Maupassant) gets a brief mention. Furthermore although three of the stories here are only simple dramatic sketches, in the others Maupassant introduces memorable descriptions of the countryside, the places where the events happened and the atmosphere surrounding them. Maupassant's mind in common with many 'naturalistic' writers of his generation was like a camera; it took in pictures which he brilliantly reproduces in words and phrases.

Although these stories were written well over a century ago and the society in which Maupassant was living was very different to that of to-day; they still seem remarkably relevant. Maupassant was never married. Some people have wrongly described him as a misogynist, others as a mere journalist. Some of his stories are cruel, others sad, some cynical, others hilarious and they are all enjoyable.

ACKNOWLEDGEMENTS

I am greatly indebted to the biography of Maupassant written by Nadine Satiat and published by Flammarion in 2003. Also my sincere thanks are due to Gallimard and the Folio Classique series of Maupassant's short stories and to the authors of the notes to the texts. Finally I would not have been able to self-publish this book without the devoted help of Inge Work Clausen who reproduced the manuscript on her computer and the assistance of Michael Chesworth who kindly corrected the proofs.

THE RONDOLI SISTERS

I

"No", said Pierre Jouvenet, "I don't know Italy and yet twice I've tried to go there. But each time I found myself held up not far from the frontier in such a way that it was always impossible for me to proceed much further. Yet those two attempts have given me a charming insight into the customs of that beautiful country. All I have to do now is to become familiar with the cities, the museums and the masterpieces which flourish there. But at the first opportunity I will try again to venture forth into that unexplored territory."

"You don't understand? Let me explain."

*

It was in 1874 that I felt that I wanted to see Venice, Florence, Rome and Naples. The idea came to me round about the 15th June when the powerful sap of springtime kindles in one's heart the excitements of love and travel.

However I am not a traveller. Moving from place to place seems to me to be a useless and tiring activity. The nights on the train when one's sleep is shattered by the rumbling of the carriages, the headaches, the aching limbs, the waking up exhausted in that box on wheels, the grime on the skin, the smuts that fly into one's eyes and hair, the stench of smoke in the throat, the ghastly meals in draughty buffets – in my opinion all these things make for a hateful beginning to a pleasant trip.

After this introduction on the 'Express', we have the depressing hotel, the big hotel full of people yet so empty, the discouraging and unfamiliar room, the dubious bed.

I prefer my own bed more than anything. It is the sanctuary of life. I get into it with a naked and weary body to be refreshed and rested in the whiteness of its sheets and the warmth of the duvets.

It is there that we find the sweetest hours of existence, the hours of love and sleep. The bed is sacred. It must be respected, venerated and loved by us as the best and dearest possession on earth.

I cannot lift up the sheet of a hotel bed without a shiver of disgust. What went on there the other night? What unwashed and repulsive people have slept on this mattress? And I think of all those frightful types with whom we come into contact daily, their nasty deformities, their spotty skin, their dirty hands which makes us think of their feet and other unmentionables. I am reminded of the people one meets in the street who put up one's nose either the revolting smell of garlic or humanity; I think of the infirmities, the infections and the sweat of ill people, of all the ugliness and obscenities of mankind.

All that has been experienced in this bed on which I was going to sleep. As I slip my feet inside, my heart sinks.

Furthermore those hotel dinners, those long table d'hôte dinners surrounded by all those tiresome ridiculous people; and also those awful solitary restaurant meals at a little table facing a miserable candle and lampshade!

And the depressing evenings in an unknown city? Do you know anything more ghastly than nightfall in a foreign town? We go forward in a crowd, an agitation which seems unreal as if in a dream. We see faces which we have never set eyes on before and will never see again. We listen to voices talking of things which are of no concern to us in a language we do not even understand…. . We experience the dreadful sensation of being lost. Our heart sinks, our knees are weak and our spirit is crushed. We walk on to escape going back to the hotel, where again we would feel even more lost because we would be at home, a home which everybody pays for. So we end up by slumping on a chair in a garish café whose décor and lighting bear down on us a thousand times worse than the shadows in the street. Then in front of a dripping glass of beer brought by a running waiter, we feel so terribly lonely that a kind of madness seizes us , an urgent need to leave, to get somewhere else, no matter where, anything to avoid staying at that marble table and under those glaring lights. And suddenly we are aware that always and everywhere in the world we really are alone and even in familiar places known contacts only give an illusion of human brotherhood. It is during these lost hours, in black isolation in far off cities when we think clearly, profoundly, and easily. It is then that we really see life with a single glance outside the vision of eternal hope, away from the accepted false conventions, away from continual dreams of expected happiness.

It is by going far away that we really understand how everything is close by, short term, meaningless; it is by seeking the unknown that we realise how every thing is mediocre and quickly over; it is by travelling the world that we find how small it is and constantly practically the same.

Oh! The dark evenings walking haphazardly through unknown streets, I recognise them and fear them most of all.

So since nothing would induce me to leave for a trip to Italy alone, I decided to get my friend, Paul Pavilly, to accompany me.

You know Paul, for him, the world, life, it is women. For him existence itself is a poem illuminated by the presence of women. The earth is only habitable because they are there; the sun is warm and bright because it shines on them. The air is sweet to breathe because it passes lightly over their skin and ruffles the hair on their temples. The moon is wonderful because it makes them dream and lends to love a languid charm. To be sure women are the motive for all Paul's actions; all his thoughts are directed towards them as well as all his efforts and all his hopes.

A poet has branded this type of man:

Most of all I loathe the bard who with tearful eye
Looks at a star while murmuring a name,
For him the vast heavens would be empty
If Lisette or Ninon were not riding behind.

Those people are so charming who take the pain
To get interested in this poor world
But tie some skirts to the trees on the plain
And a white bonnet to the brow of green hillsides.

For sure they've not understood thy music divine
Eternal nature with the trembling voice,
Those who don't go alone through deep ravines
But dream of a woman with the noise of the trees.[1]

When I spoke to Paul about Italy, at first he absolutely refused to leave Paris, But I told him some stories of travel adventures and explained how charming Italian women were; I held out hopes to him of delicate pleasures in Naples thanks to a recommendation I had from certain signor Michel Amoroso whose connections were extremely useful to tourists; so he allowed himself to be tempted.

II

We took the Express one Thursday evening 26th June. At that time hardly anyone went down to the Midi. We were alone in the compartment, both of us in a bad temper, annoyed at leaving Paris, and deploring that we had given in to this tourist idea; we regretted the freshness of Marly, the beauty of the Seine, the pleasant riverside; we regretted the good days of messing about in a boat, and the good evenings lazing about on the bank waiting for nightfall.

Paul was slumped in a corner and as soon as the train started, he declared:

"It is stupid to go down there."

Since it was too late for him to change his mind, I replied: "You need not have come."

He did not answer. But seeing his furious expression, I wanted to laugh. Certainly he resembled a squirrel. Incidentally each of us reveals in our features, underlying the human form, a species of animal as the mark of our primitive ancestry. How many people have the mouth of a bulldog, the head of a goat, a rabbit, a fox, a horse, an ox! Paul was a squirrel transformed into a man. He had the animal's darting eyes, the reddish hair, the pointed nose, the slim little body which is supple and active; and an odd resemblance to its general behaviour. How do I know? I would say that the similarity of gestures, movements and mannerisms was remarkable.

At last we both fell asleep, that fitful sleep on a train interrupted by sudden halts producing horrible cramps in the arms and neck.

We woke when the train was rattling along beside the Rhone. Soon the continuous chirping of cicadas came through the window, that chirping which seems to be the voice of warm earth, the song of Provence; the noise hit us in the face, in the chest, in the soul, that joyful atmosphere of the Midi, the smell of burnt ground, the bright rocky countryside, the stunted olive trees with grey-green foliage.

As the train stopped again, an official ran along the length of the carriages shouting 'Valence' at the top of his voice. 'Valence'! It was a real 'Valence', with the accent, exactly the accent which finally confirmed for us the sensation of Provence which the discordant note of the cicadas had already given us.

As far as Marseille, nothing new.

We got down from the train and went to the buffet for something to eat.

When we climbed back into our compartment a woman was settled in there.

Paul glanced at me in delight; with a mechanical gesture he twirled his small moustache; next ruffling it a little, he ran his fingers through his hair like a comb; it had been very messed up by a night on the train. Then he sat down facing the stranger.

Every time I find myself in front of a new face, maybe on a journey, maybe in a crowd I have an obsession to try and guess what character, what intellect, what mind lies behind the features.

She was a young woman, quite young and pretty and certainly a girl from the Midi. She had superb eyes, marvellous black wavy hair which was slightly curly; it was so luxurious and long that if anything it gave an impression of a weight on her head; elegantly dressed with a certain southern poor taste, she seemed a bit common. The proportions of her face did not have that perfection of dignified breeding, that refinement which sons of aristocrats acquire at birth and which is the hereditary mark of different blood.

She wore bracelets which were too large to be of gold and earrings decorated with transparent stones too big to be diamonds. In her whole person somehow or other she was uncultured. I guessed that she would talk too loudly and shout at every opportunity, gesticulating with exuberance.

The train departed.

She remained motionless in her seat, staring straight in front of her in the sullen posture of a furious woman.

Paul started to chat to me, talking of things designed to produce an effect, arranging the conversation to attract attention like shopkeepers lay out and show their choicest wares to arouse interest.

But she seemed not to be listening.

"Toulon! Ten minutes stop! Buffet!" cried the guard.

Paul motioned to me to get down and as soon as we were on the platform:

"Tell me what do you make of her?"

I started to laugh. "Me, I've no idea. I'm easy."

He was very fired up: "She is devilishly pretty and fresh, the bird. What eyes! But she seems unhappy; she must have a problem. She is paying no attention."

"You are wasting your time," I murmured.

But he was annoyed: "My dear chap, I'm not making the running, I find the lady attractive, that's all; – if one could talk to her? But what to say? Let's see, you, have you any ideas? Have you an inkling of what she might be?"

"Good Lord, no; however I would be inclined to say – a minor actress rejoining her troupe after an amorous escapade."

He had a shocked air as if I had said something hurtful, and he replied: "How do you make that out? On the contrary, personally, I find that she looks very correct."

I answered: "Look at the bracelets, old boy, and the earrings and the outfit. I wouldn't be at all surprised if she was a dancer, or perhaps even a circus girl, but rather a dancer. She has something about her which smacks of the theatre."

That idea definitely upset him: "My dear fellow, she is too young. She is hardly twenty."

"But, old boy, there are plenty of things one can do before the age of twenty. Dancing and reciting are some examples without counting on some other things which she perhaps practises exclusively."

"Passengers for the Nice Express, Vintmille – on the train!" shouted the guard.

It was time to reboard. Our neighbour was eating an orange. Really she did not have a genteel approach. She had spread her handkerchief on her knees; her method of peeling the golden skin, of opening her mouth to take the segments between her lips, and of splitting the pips through the window illustrated perfectly a common upbringing in the matter of behaviour and manners.

Also she seemed more disgruntled than ever and the furious way she was swallowing her fruit was quite funny.

Paul was looking at her passionately, searching for what was needed to attract her attention and arouse her curiosity. Then he started to chat to me again, mentioning a whole procession of brilliant ideas and quoting well known names in a familiar way. But she took no notice whatsoever of his efforts.

We went through Frejus and Saint-Raphael. The train was passing through this garden; it was a paradise of roses, a forest of blossoming orange and lemon trees which was showing off both their white sprays and their golden fruit in this kingdom of perfume; all along this marvellous coast running from Marseille to Genoa it was a country of flowers.

It is during June that you must follow this coastline; all the most beautiful flowers are growing wild along the narrow valleys, on the hillsides; over and over again you can see roses, fields, hedges and thickets of roses. They climb walls, advance across rooftops and scale trees; they burst out white, red and yellow, big and small; their foliage is thin like a dress which is simple and plain or thick like clothing which is heavy and glossy.

Their powerful scents continuously fills the air, rendering it languid and appetising, and the more penetrating scent of the orange blossom seems to sweeten the air you breathe turning it into sugar for the nostrils.

Bathed by the placid Mediterranean, the huge coast of dark rocks stretches into the distance. The strong summer sunshine falls in a golden sheet on the mountains, on the long sandy beaches and on the azure and motionless sea. The train runs on, enters tunnels to pass under peaks and slides round curves in the hills; it crosses over the sea on a narrow cornice as if on a wall; a sweet and slightly salty tang of drying seaweed sometimes mingles with the strong and exciting scent of flowers.

But Paul was seeing nothing and smelling nothing. Our neighbour was occupying all his attention.

At Cannes, he had to speak to me again and motioned to me to get down from the train.

He had hardly made our exit when he took my arm:

"You know, she is ravishing; Look at her eyes and her hair, my dear chap. I've never seen the like!"

I told him: "Come on, calm down; or, better, make a pass if you want to. She doesn't see to be impregnable, although she appears a little disgruntled."

He replied: "Can you talk to her? Me, I am tongue-tied. At the start, I am idiotically shy. I never know how to approach a girl in the street. I follow them and turn round; I come close and I never discover the right words. Only once have I made an attempt at conversation; that was once when I noticed that my approaches were obviously expected and it was absolutely vital to say something, I stammered: "How are you, Madame?" She laughed in my face and I rushed off."

I promised Paul to use all my skill to start a conversation, and when we had regained our seats, politely I asked our neighbour:

"Does tobacco smoke upset you, Madame?"

She replied: "Non capisco."[(2)]

She was Italian! I had a crazy urge to laugh. Paul did not know a word of the language and I would have to act as an interpreter. I started to play my part. So I announced in Italian:

"I was asking you, Madame, if tobacco smoke in any way embarrasses you?"

With a furious gesture, she threw me: "Che mi fa!"[(3)]

She had neither turned her head nor looked up at me and I was very taken aback, not knowing if I should take that "What's it got to do with me" for an authorisation or a refusal, for a real sign of indifference, or for a simple "Leave me in peace."

I repeated: "Madame, if the smell embarrasses you in the remotest way?"

Then she answered: "Mica"[(4)] in a tone of voice which was equivalent to: "Clear off!" It was, nevertheless, a permission and I said to Paul: "You may smoke." He gave me the astonished look which one has when trying to understand a person speaking a foreign language in one's presence and he asked me in rather an odd way:

"What did you say to her?"

"I asked her if we could smoke."

"Then she doesn't understand French?"

"Not a word."

"What did she say?"

"That she authorised us to do as we pleased."

I lit my cigar.

Paul went on: "Is that all she said?"

"My dear chap, if you had counted her words, you would have noticed that she pronounced just six, including two to make one realise that she did not speak French. So in four words, one cannot really express a number of things."

Paul seemed disorientated, disappointed and quite unhappy.

But suddenly our Italian neighbour asked in the same discontented tone which seemed normal to her: "Do you know when we will arrive in Genoa?"

I replied: "At 11 o'clock this evening, Madame." Then, after a minute of silence, I went on: "My friend and I, we are also going to Genoa and if, during the journey, we could be useful to you for something, believe me we would be very happy."

As she did not answer I insisted: "You are alone and if you have need of our services ….." She uttered a new: "Mica" so firmly that I shut up quickly.

Paul asked:

"What did she say?"

"She said that she found you charming."

But he was not in the mood for joking and drily begged me not to make fun of him. Then I translated the young woman's question and my gallant proposition so crudely repulsed.

He was really agitated like a squirrel in a cage; he said: "If we could know what hotel she has booked we can go to the same one; so try to question her cleverly to give us another opportunity to talk to her."

Really it was not easy; I did not know what to invent and I was also keen to get to know this difficult person.

We passed through Nice, Monaco, Menton and then stopped at the frontier for a luggage check.

Although I have a horror of badly brought up people who picnic and eat in a railway carriage, I went off to buy a load of provisions in a supreme effort to tempt the appetite of our companion. I sensed that in normal times at first this girl would be easy. Some sort of problem was making her irritable, but perhaps it was really nothing at all and a desire awakened, a word, a careful suggestion would be enough to soothe her worries, placate her and win her over.

We departed again. We were still all three of us alone in the compartment. I spread out my picnic on the seat; I cut up the chicken and neatly laid out the slices of ham on the paper, then quite near the young woman I nicely arranged our dessert: strawberries, plums, cherries and sweets.

When she saw what we were starting to eat, she in her turn pulled out some chocolate and two croissants from a little bag, and with her beautiful fine teeth she started to munch the chocolate bar and crispy bread.

Paul said to me in an undertone:

"Well, invite her then!"

"It is exactly my intention, my dear chap, but the introduction is not easy."

However, occasionally she was looking over our picnic and I felt sure that she would still be hungry after she had eaten her two croissants. So I let her finish her frugal meal. Then I asked her:

"You will be quite welcome, Madame, if you would like to accept some of this fruit?"

Again she replied: "Mica" but in a voice which was less disagreeable than earlier in the day, and I continued to insist: "Then will you allow me to offer you a little wine. I see you have drunk nothing. It is the wine of your country; since we are now in Italy we would be extremely pleased to see a pretty Italian mouth accept the offer of Frenchmen, your neighbours."

She said: "No" with a gentle shake of her head having both the will to refuse and the wish to accept; again she said: "Mica" but it was a 'Mica' which was almost polite. I took the bottle in its straw case, Italian fashion; I filled a glass and presented it to her.

"Drink," I said to her "this will be our welcome in your country."

She took the glass with a disconcerted air and swallowed the wine with one gulp, like a woman tortured with thirst; then she handed it back to me without even a thank you.

Then I presented the cherries: "Take them, Madame, please. You can see that you are making us very happy."

From her corner she looked at the fruit spread out beside her and then spoke so rapidly that I had great difficulty in following her: 'A me non piacciono ne le ciliegie ne le susine; amo soltanto le fragole'.

"What is she saying?" asked Paul immediately.

"She said that she doesn't like the cherries or the plums but only the strawberries."

Then I placed the newspaper full of wild strawberries on her knees. Straightaway she began to eat them very quickly, holding them between her fingers and popping them into her mouth in a manner which was both charming and coquettish.

As soon as she had finished the little red heap which we had seen melt away and disappear in a few minutes under the lively movements of her hands, I asked her: "And now what can I offer you?"

She replied: "I would like a little chicken."

And she devoured certainly half the chicken which she tore apart like a carnivorous animal with big bites of her jaw. Next she decided to have some cherries which she said she did not like, then some plums and then some cakes. Finally she said: "That is enough" and she curled up in her corner.

I was beginning to enjoy myself very much and I wanted to make her eat more, multiplying my offers and compliments to persuade her. But suddenly again she became furious and hurled in my face a repeated 'Mica' in such a terrible way that I did not risk bothering her digestion any more.

I turned to my friend: "My poor Paul, I think we are wasting our time."

Night came, a hot summer's night which arrived slowly extending its warm shadows over the shimmering and tired earth. A long way off over the sea lights shone out from place to place

– on promontories and on tops of headlands; stars began to show up on the darkened horizon and sometimes I confused them with the lighthouses.

The perfume of the orange trees grew more intense; drunkenly we breathed it in, swelling our lungs to drink it in deeply. Something sweet, delicious and divine seemed to be floating in the balmy air.

Suddenly under the trees, alongside the track I spotted in the now completely dark shadows something like a shower of stars. One could say that these drops of darting light, flitting, running and playing in the leaves were like stars which had fallen from the sky to hold a party on earth. They were the fireflies dancing a strange flickering ballet in the perfumed air.

By chance one of them came into our compartment and started to buzz around with its winking light. I put the blue shade over our lamp and watched this fantastic fly following its glowing flight; suddenly it settled on the black hair of our neighbour who was dozing after her meal. Paul was ecstatic; his eyes were fixed on this brilliant speck which scintillated like a sparkling jewel on the brow of the sleeping girl.

The Italian girl awoke around a quarter to eleven still carrying the little flaming insect in her hair. Seeing her stirring, I said to her: "We are arriving at Genoa, Madame." Without answering me, she muttered as if obsessed by a fixed and embarrassing thought: 'What am I going to do now?'

Then suddenly she asked me:

"Would you like me to come with you?"

I was so amazed that I did not understand.

"How – with us? What do you mean?"

She repeated with an air which became more and more furious:

"Do you want me to go with you straightaway?"

"Yes, I do, but where do you wish to go? Where would you like me to take you?"

She shrugged her shoulders with haughty indifference.

"Whatever you want! It makes no difference to me."

Twice she repeated: "Che mi fa?"

"But we are going to the hotel?"

She said in the most scornful tone: "All right then! Let's go to the hotel."

I turned towards Paul and announced:

"She is asking if we would like her to come with us."

The flustered surprise of my friend allowed me to recover my composure. He stammered:

"With us? Where? How? Why?"

"Me, I have no idea. She has just made me this strange proposition in the most irritable tone. I said that we were going to the hotel and she replied: 'Very well then. Let's go to the hotel!' She can't have a sou. I am easy. She has an odd way of introducing herself."

Trembling and agitated, Paul exclaimed: "But, certainly, yes. I'm keen. Tell her that we will give her a lift wherever she wants." Then he hesitated a second and continued in an anxious voice: "Only we will need to know with whom she is coming? Will it be you or me?"

I turned towards the girl who did not even seem to be listening and was showing a complete lack of interest. I said: "We would be delighted, Madame, to take you with us. Only my friend wishes to know whether you will be taking my arm or his?"

She turned her large dark eyes on me and answered in vague surprise: "Che mi fa?"

I explained: "In Italy, I believe, you call a friend who takes care of all the desires of a woman, who looks after all her needs, and satisfies all her whims a 'parito'. Which of us two do you want to be your 'parito'?"

She replied without hesitation: "You!"

I turned back towards Paul: "It is me she has chosen, my dear chap, you are out of luck."

In a rage he declared: "So much the better for you."

Then after several minutes reflection, he said: "Are you set on taking that tart with us? She is going to make us miss our trip.

What do you think we are going to do with a woman with an air of 'I don't know what'? They are not going to accept us in a proper hotel, that's obvious!"

But I was just beginning to find the Italian girl much better than I had first judged ….. Yes, I was definitely set on taking her now. I was even delighted with the thought, and I was already feeling those little tremors of anticipation which the prospect of a night of love making induces in the blood.

I replied: "Look, old boy, we have accepted. It is too late to back out. You were the first to advise me to say yes."

He grumbled: "It is stupid! All right, do as you wish."

The train whistled and slowed down; we had arrived.

I got down from the carriage and then offered a hand to my new companion. She jumped lightly down and I gave her my arm which she appeared to take with distaste. Once the luggage had been identified and reclaimed, we set off across the town. Paul was walking in silence with a nervous step.

I said to him: "Which hotel are we going to descend on? Perhaps it is awkward to go to the 'Cité of Paris' with a woman, especially with this Italian."

Paul interrupted me: "Yes with an Italian who looks more like a tart than a duchess. All right, that doesn't concern me. Do as you please!"

I was hesitant. I had written to the 'Cité of Paris' to reserve our suite ….. and now ….. I did not know any longer what to decide. Two porters were following us with the suitcases. I continued to Paul: "You should go well on ahead to tell them we have arrived. Also will you let the manager know that I am following with ….. a friend, and we want a suite with three rooms quite separate. This is so as not to mingle with other tourists. He will understand and we will make up our minds after his response."

But Paul grumbled: "Thanks, these commissions and this role hardly suit me. I have not come here to prepare your rooms and your pleasures."

I insisted: "Look, my dear chap, don't get annoyed. Surely it is better to get into a good hotel than a bad one and it is really not difficult to go and ask the manager for three separate rooms and a dining room."

I emphasised the three which decided him.

So he went on ahead and I saw him go through the main entrance of the fine hotel while I remained on the other side of the street dragging my dumb Italian and followed by the porters close behind with the luggage….

Finally Paul came back with a face as gloomy as that of my companion: "It is done," he said, "they have accepted us; but there are only two rooms. You will organise yourself as best you can."

I followed him in, ashamed to enter with this suspect company.

In fact we had two rooms divided by a small living room. I requested that they bring us a cold supper and then I turned, a little hesitant towards my companion.

"We have only been able to take two rooms, Madame. Will you choose which one you would like?"

She replied with the eternal 'che mi fa?' Then I picked up off the the floor her little black wooden chest – a true servant's suitcase and carried it into the right hand room which I chose for her ….. for us. A French hand had written on a stuck on square label: 'Mademoiselle Francesca Rondoli Genoa'.

I asked: "Your name is Francesca?"

She nodded her head without replying.

I went on: "We are going to have supper presently. Meanwhile perhaps you would like to have a wash?"

She replied with a 'Mica' which was a word she used as often as the 'Che mi fa'. I insisted: "After a train journey, it is so pleasant to get cleaned up."

Then I had an idea that perhaps she did not have with her all those essential things that a woman needs; surely she seemed to be in a special situation like having just escaped some unpleasant affair. I brought her my wash bag.

I reached for all the little personal items it contained – a nail brush, a new toothbrush – I always have an assortment with me

– my scissors, my nail files and my sponges. I uncorked a flask of eau de cologne, a flask of amber lavender water and a little bottle of newmown hay, in order to give her the choice. I opened my box of rice powder where my light powder puff was immersed. I placed one of my fine towels over the water jug and a new bar of soap near the basin.

She was following my movements, wide eyed and angry. She did not seem either surprised or satisfied with my attentions.

I said to her: "There you are, everything you need. I will let you know when the supper is ready."

I retired to the living room. Paul had taken possession of the other bedroom and had locked the door. So I was left alone to wait.

A waiter came and went bringing plates and glasses. He set the table slowly and then put down cold chicken. He announced that the supper was served.

I knocked gently on Mlle Rondoli's door. She shouted: "Come in." I entered. A suffocating odour of perfume hit me, that heavy, penetrating odour of a hairdressing saloon.

The girl was sitting on her box, in the attitude of a disgruntled dreamer or a housemaid who has been given the sack. Immediately I appreciated what she might have meant by doing her toilette. The towel had stayed folded over the water jug which was still full; the soap, untouched and dry remained by the basin; on the other hand one might say that the young woman had drunk half of the flasks of toilet water; however she had been careful with the eau de cologne; only a third of the bottle was missing; to make up for that she had consumed a surprising amount of amber lavender water and newmown hay. As for the face powder, she had applied so much of it to her face and neck that a cloud of it seemed to be drifting in the air. She was carrying a sort of snow on her eyelids, eyebrows and temples and deep layers could be seen plastered on the hollows of her face, the sides of her nose, in the dimple on her chin and in the corner of her eyes.

When she got up she exuded such a terrible odour that I felt a migraine coming on.

We sat down to supper. Paul was in an abominable temper. I could only draw from him words of blame, irritated observations or unpleasant compliments.

Mlle Francesca ate ravenously. As soon as she had finished her meal, she dozed off on the sofa. However I anxiously saw the decisive moment coming – the sharing of bedrooms. I determined to force the issue and sitting next to the girl I gallantly kissed her hand.

Wearily she opened her eyes and beneath her dropping lids she gave me a sleepy and always disgruntled look.

I said to her: "Since we only have two bedrooms, will you allow me to share yours?"

She replied: "Please yourself. I'm easy. Che mi fa?"

This indifference hurt me: "So you will not be upset if I go with you?"

"Do what you want. It makes no difference to me."

"Do you want to go to bed straightaway?"

"Yes, please, I am sleepy."

She got up, yawned and offered her hand to Paul who took it in a fury. I lit the lamp in her room.

But a worry was haunting me: "Here is," I told her again, "everything you need."

And I took the trouble myself to pour half the jug of water into the basin and to place the towel near the soap.

Then I went back to Paul. As soon as I had come in, he declared: "You have got a right cow there!"

Laughing I replied: "My dear chap, do not criticise grapes which are none too ripe."

He answered with wicked snigger: "You will find out about that, old boy, if she gives you the pox."

I started; I was seized by that gnawing fear, that fear which pursues us after suspect affairs, the fear which spoils delightful encounters, unforeseen caresses, and stolen kisses. However I put brave face to it: "Go on, this girl is not a tramp."

But he pressed on, the beggar! He had seen the shadow of anxiety cross my face: "For all you know about her I find you amazing! You pick up an Italian girl travelling alone on the train. Very cynically she offers to sleep with you in the first hotel you come to. You take her in and you consider that she is not a tart! And you persuade yourself that you will be running no more risk tonight than if you were going to spend the night in bed with a woman known to be infected with the pox."

He was shaking with angry and vulgar laughter.

I sat down, tortured with worry. What was I going to do? He was right and as for me there was a terrible conflict between fear and desire.

He went on: "Please yourself. I have warned you; you will not complain of the consequences."

But I saw in his eyes such ironic amusement, such pleasure in his revenge; he was having such a joke at my expense that I hesitated no longer. I shook his hand and said: "Good night."

'To conquer without danger, is to triumph without glory.' [5]

"And, by God, old boy, the victory is worth the risk."

And I entered Francesca's room with a firm step.

I stopped at the door, surprised and amazed. She was already asleep stark naked on the bed. Sleep had overtaken her just as she was getting undressed and she was laying in the charming pose of Titian's famous lady. [6]

It seemed that she had lain down out of weariness to take off her stockings since they had remained on the sheet. Then she had thought of something, obviously something pleasant, because to finish her reverie she had waited a little before getting up; then gently closing her eyes she had lost consciousness. A nightdress, embroidered at the neck, purchased in a ready to wear shop, expensive for a debutant, was draped across a chair.

She was charming, young, cool and firm.

What is prettier than a woman asleep? All the sweet contours of the body, all its seductive curves, all its soft features which trouble the heart seem designed for immobility on the bed; that undulating line which becomes hollow at the side, then rises at the hip and then falls with the light and smooth slope of the leg to finish so coquettishly at the end of the foot is really only depicted with all its charm when stretched out on the sheets of a couch.

In a second I was going to forget all the sound advice of my comrade; but, turning suddenly towards the dressing table, I saw everything in the same state where I had left them. I sat down very anxiously and tormented by indecision.

Certainly I stayed seated a long time, a very long time, perhaps an hour without deciding anything – whether to be bold or to escape. Besides withdrawal was impossible; it was necessary maybe to spend the night in a chair, maybe to lie down in my turn at my own risk and peril.

As for sleeping where I was or in the bed, inevitably I did not think about it. My brain was too agitated and my eyes too occupied.

I stirred continuously, restless, feverishly, ill at ease, and excessively nervous. Then I made a reasoned decision to capitulate; "I am not committed to anything if I lie down. To relax it will always be better for me on a mattress than in a chair."

So I got undressed slowly; then getting over the sleeping girl, I stretched out against the wall, offering my back to temptation.

And again I stayed like that a long time, a very long time without sleeping.

But suddenly my neighbour awoke. She opened her eyes, astonished and still discontented. Then realising that she was naked, she got up and calmly put on her nightdress with as much indifference as if I had not been there.

Then …. Good God ….. I took advantage of the situation, without her, needless to say, appearing to have the slightest concern in the world. Then she went to sleep again with her head resting on her right arm.

And I began to muse on the rashness of human beings. Then finally I dozed off.

She got dressed early like a woman accustomed to work in the mornings. The movements she made getting up woke me and I watched her through half closed eyelids.

She came and went without being hurried, as if astonished at having nothing to do. Then she decided to go back to the dressing table and in a minute she emptied what was left of the perfumes in the flasks. She also used some water but not much.

Next when she was completely dressed, she sat down again on her box, clasping one knee in her hands and looking thoughtful.

Then I made it appear that I had just seen her and I said: "Good morning, Francesca."

Without seeming any more gracious than the evening before, she pouted: "Good morning."

I asked: "Have you slept well?"

She nodded without answering; and jumping out of bed, I went forward to kiss her.

She held out her face to me with the annoyed gesture of a spoilt child. Then I took her tenderly in my arms (the wine being uncorked I would be truly stupid not to drink more) and I slowly placed my lips on her large flashing eyes which she closed out of boredom under my kisses, then on her bright cheeks and on her full lips which she turned away.

I said to her: "So you don't like it when someone kisses you?"

She replied: "Mica."

I sat down on the box beside her, putting my arm through hers: "Mica! Mica! Mica! To everything. From now on I am going to call you only Mlle Mica."

For the first time, I thought I saw a shadow of a smile on her lips but it went so quickly that I could well have been mistaken.

"But if you always reply 'mica' I shall no longer know what to do to try and please you. Let's see, today, what are we going to do?"

She hesitated as if a hint of a wish had entered her head, then nonchalantly she announced: "I'm easy. Please yourself."

"All right, mademoiselle Mica, we will take a carriage and we will go for a walk."

She murmured: "As you wish."

Paul was waiting for us in the dining room with the bored expression of a third party in a love affair. I put on a delighted smile and shook his hand heartily in admission of triumph.

I replied: "First we will pay a little visit to the town and then we can take a carriage to some corner of the outskirts."

Breakfast was taken in silence. Then we departed through the streets to visit the museums. I trailed Francesca on my arm from palace to palace. We did the Spinola Palace, the Doria, the Marcello Durazzo, the Red Palace and the White Palace. She didn't look at anything or rather occasionally she glanced at a masterpiece with a nonchalant and lethargic eye. Paul was very annoyed and followed us, muttering and making unpleasant remarks. Next we had a drive through the countryside in the carriage during which all three of us remained silent.

Then we returned for dinner.

The next day it was the same thing and the day after.

On the third day Paul said to me: "You know me, I'm clearing off, I am not going to hang around for three weeks watching you making love with that tart."

I was totally taken aback and very embarrassed; for to my huge surprise I was hooked on Francesca in a remarkable fashion. A man is weak and foolish, swept off by anything, a coward every time he is feeling excited or crushed. I stuck to this girl whom I did not know, this discontented and taciturn creature. I loved her disgruntled expression, her pouting mouth, her bored look. I loved her lethargic gestures, her scornful consent; I even went as far as loving the indifference of her caresses. A secret bond, that mysterious bond of bestial love, that intimacy of unsatisfied possession kept me close to her. I said as much to Paul quite frankly. He treated me like an imbecile and then said: "Oh well, take her then."

But obstinately she refused to leave Genoa and would not explain why. I used prayers, arguments and promises. Nothing worked.

And so I was staying.

Paul declared that he was going to leave on his own. He even packed his suitcase, but he also stayed.

Fifteen days went by.

Francesca always taciturn and in a terrible temper lived at my side rather than with me. She responded to all my requests, all my wishes and all my proposals with her eternal 'Che mi fa' and her no les 'eternal 'mica'.

My friend did not simmer down. To all his fits of anger, I used to reply: "You can go away if you are annoyed. I'm not keeping you."

Then he used to swear at me, lambasting me with his approaches shouting: "But where do you think I can go now? We had three weeks at our disposal, and, look, fifteen days have gone already! And then, as if I was going to leave all alone for Venice, Florence and Rome! But you will pay me for it and more than you think. You cannot make a man come all the way from Paris to coop him up in a hotel with an Italian tramp!"

I used to say to him quietly: "Oh well, return to Paris then." And he used to shout: "I am going to do just that and no later than tomorrow."

But the next day he stayed like the day before always swearing and furious.

People recognised us in the streets where we wandered from morning to evening; there were no pavements in the narrow streets of this town which resembled an immense stone labyrinth pierced with corridors like underground passages; we went through these passages where there were furious currents of air, and also in enclosed side streets between walls which were so high that one could hardly see the sky. Occasionally some French people would turn round, astonished to recognise fellow countrymen in the company of this bored girl with a revealing dress, whose appearance between us was singularly and scandalously out of place.

She went along, totally disinterested, leaning on my arm. Why was she hanging on to me, with us, who were apparently giving her so little pleasure? Who was she? Where did she come from? What was she doing? Did she have a project or an idea? Or rather was she there for the adventure, for the chance encounter? I searched in vain to get to the bottom of it, to explain it, to understand her. The more I got to know her, the more she amazed me and the more she seemed like an enigma. She was certainly no slut, making love her profession. She seemed to me to be more like some daughter of poor parents, seduced, trapped, then abandoned and now lost. But what did she count on becoming? What was she expecting? For in no way did she seem set on conquering me or drawing from me any real profit.

I tried to question her, to speak to her of her childhood. There was no response. I stayed with her with a free heart and a gnawing lust, never tired of holding her in my arms, this difficult and proud female: I was mated like an animal, enamoured, or rather seduced, subdued by a kind of sensual charm, a young, healthy and potent charm which she exuded from her appetising skin and the robust shape of her figure.

Another eight days went by; the end of my trip was approaching. I had to be back in Paris on 11th July. Now Paul was getting a little more involved in the plans – in just the same way continually insulting and pestering me. For my part I was always thinking up diversions, distractions, outings to amuse my mistress and my friend; I was going to endless trouble.

One day I proposed an excursion to Santa Margarita; this charming small town, surrounded by gardens, was hidden at the foot of a hillside which stretched far out to sea right up to the village of Portofino. All three of us were following the marvellous road which ran alongside the mountain. Suddenly Francesca said to me: "Tomorrow I will not be able to go out with you. I am going to see my parents."

Then she was silent. I did not question her. I was sure that she would not reply.

In fact the next day, she rose very early. Then since I was still lying down, she sat down on the end of the bed and in an embarrassed, hesitant and defiant tone she announced: "If I do not come back this evening, will you come and fetch me?"

I replied: "But of course. Where should I go?"

She explained: "You go into Victor Emmanuel Street, then you take the Falcon passage and the Saint-Raphael side street;

you will go into the furniture shop and in the courtyard right at the back, in the building which is to the right you ask for Madame Rondoli; it is there."

And she left. I remained considerably surprised.

On seeing me alone, Paul was stunned and stammered: "So where is Francesca?" I told him what had just happened.

He cried out: "Oh well, my dear chap, take advantage of the opportunity and let's clear off. Also, look, our time is well up. Two days more or less will change nothing. Let's get going, on the road, pack your case, let's get on our way!"

I refused: "But no, old boy, I really cannot chuck this girl in such a fashion after spending nearly three weeks with her. I must say good-bye and get her to accept something; no, I will not behave like a swine."

But he did not want to listen; he pressed and harassed me but I was not giving in.

I did not go out during the day expecting Francisca to return. She did not come back.

In the evening, at dinner, Paul was triumphant: "It is her who has chucked you, old boy; that's funny, really fanny."

I admit that I was astonished and a little upset. He was laughing in my face and mocking me: "Incidentally the method isn't bad, although primitive: "Expect me, I am coming back."

"Are you going to wait for her a long time? Who knows? Perhaps you might have the naiveté to go and look for her at the address given: "Madame Rondoli please? – It is not here sir." I bet you would like to go there?"

I protested: "But no, my dear fellow, and I assure you that if she has not returned by tomorrow morning, I will leave on the eight o'clock express. I will have stayed twenty-four hours. It is enough. My conscience will be clear."

I spent the whole evening worrying, a little sad, a little nervous. Truly in my heart I had something going for her. At midnight I went to bed. I hardly slept.

I was up at six o'clock. I woke Paul and packed my suitcase. Two hours later, together, we caught the train for France.

III

The following year just at the same time it happened that I was struck as one is by a recurring illness, by a new desire to see Italy. I decided right away to undertake the journey – to visit Florence, Venice and Rome which is surely part of the education of a person who is well brought up. Besides in society it results in a multitude of topics of conversation and allows one to reel off artistic banalities which always appear profound.

This time I went alone, and I arrived in Genoa without any incident on the journey. I booked into the same hotel and by coincidence I was given the same room.

But hardly had I got into that bed when, well, the memory of Francesca, which already the evening before had been floating vaguely in my thoughts, now haunted me with a curious persistence.

Are you familiar with that obsession with a woman when, a long time afterwards you return to the place where you have loved her and slept with her?

It is one of the most violent and painful sensations that I know … It appears that you see her coming in, smiling and opening her arms. Her image, both fleeting and distinct, is in front of you; it passes, comes back and disappears. It tortures you like a nightmare, grips you, fills your mind and troubles your senses by its unreal presence. Your eye perceives her, the scent of her perfume follows you; you have the taste of her kisses on your lips and on your body the feel of her skin. Yet you are alone and you know it; you suffer from that peculiar agitation which a ghost evokes. A heavy, upsetting sadness envelopes you. It seems that you have just been abandoned for all time. All the objects in the room take on a sorrowful significance and produce in your soul, in your heart, a horrible impression of isolation and rejection. Oh! Never revisit the town, the house, the room, the wood, the gardens, the bench where you have held an adored woman in your arms.

Finally all night long I was pursued by the memory of Francesca; and little by little the desire to see her again got hold of me; at first the desire was confused, then more lively, sharper, burning. So I decided to spend the next day in Genoa to try and find her. If I did not succeed, I would take the train in the evening.

So in the morning, I set off to search for her. I remembered perfectly the details she had given on leaving me: Victor-Emmanuel Street – Falcone passage – Saint-Raphael side street, the furniture shop – the back of the courtyard, the building on the right.

Not without difficulty I found all that and knocked on the door of a kind of run down villa. A large woman came to open it; she ought to have been extremely beautiful and she was no more than extremely untidy; she was too fat, yet majestically she showed off a remarkable figure. Her dishevelled hair fell in streaks on her forehead and shoulders and one saw her huge quivering body floating in an enormous dressing gown covered with stains. Round her neck she wore a gold coloured necklace and on her wrists superb bracelets in Genoese filigree.

With an unfriendly expression she asked: "What do you want?"

I replied: "Doesn't Mlle Francesca Rondoli live here?"

"What do you want from her?"

"I had the pleasure of meeting her last year and I would like to see her again."

The old woman gave me a searching and suspicious look: "Tell me where you met her?"

"But right here in Genoa!"

"What is your name?"

I hesitated a second; then I gave my name. I'd hardly pronounced it when the Italian woman raised her arms as to kiss me: "Ah! You are the Frenchman; how happy I am to see you! How pleased! But how you have made trouble for the poor child; she waited a month for you, sir, yes, a month. From the first day she thought that you were going to come and fetch her. She wanted to see if you loved her! If you knew how she wept when she realised that you were not coming. Yes, sir, she cried her heart out. And then she went to the hotel. You had left. Then she thought that you were going to travel in Italy and that you would pass through Genoa again, and since she did not wish to go with you, you would look for her on your return. Yes, sir, she waited more than a month; and she was very sad, yes, very sad. I am her mother!"

I really felt a little upset. However I recovered my composure and asked: "Is she here just now?"

"No, sir, she is in Paris with a painter, a charming boy who loves her, sir, who loves her passionately and gives her everything she wants. Here, look what he sent me, me her mother. It is kind, isn't it"

With all her southern vivacity, she showed me the big bracelets on her arms and the heavy necklace round her throat. She went on: I also have earrings with stones, a silk dress and some rings; but I don't wear them in the morning; I only put them on occasionally when I dress up. Oh! She is very happy, sir, very happy. She will be so pleased when I write to her that you have come! But come in sir. You will have something, yes, come in."

I refused, now wanting to leave by the first train. But she had seized my arm and was pulling me, repeating: "So, come in, sir. I must tell her that you have come to our house."

And I went into the little front room which was quite dark and furnished with a table and a few chairs…

She continued: "Oh! At present she is very happy, very happy. When you met her in the train, she was very upset. Her good friend had left her in Marseille and she was coming back, the poor child. Straight away she liked you very much, but, you understand, she was still a little depressed. Now she has everything; she writes to tell me everything she does. He is called M. Bellemin. They say that he is a famous painter in your country. He met her passing through here, in the street, yes sir, in the street and he fell for her immediately. But you will have a glass of squash, yes? It is very good. Are you all alone this year?"

I replied: "Yes, I am on my own."

I felt now overtaken by a growing urge to laugh. My initial disappointment was evaporating in the face of the statements of Mme Rondoli, the mother. I needed to drink that glass of squash.

She continued: "How is it that you are all on your own? Oh! I am angry that Francesca is no longer here; she would have kept you company during the time you were staying in the town. It is not fun to go for walks on your own; and from her point of view she will regret it very much."

Then as I rose to leave, she cried: "But if you would like Carlotta to go with you, she is very familiar with the walks. She is my other girl, the second."

Doubtless she took my astonishment for consent, and she rushed towards an inside door, opened it and in the darkness of an invisible staircase, she shouted: "Carlotta! Carlotta! Come down quickly, come immediately, my darling girl."

I wanted to protest. She would not allow it: "No, she will keep you company; she is very sweet and much more fun than the other one; she is a good girl, a very good girl whom I love very much."

I heard the noise of slippers on the stairs; a fine girl, a brunette, appeared, slim and pretty but also with her hair down and under an old dress she was wearing belonging to her mother, I was able to make out her young supple body.

Mme Rondoli immediately put her in the picture as regards my situation: "It is Francisca's Frenchman, you know, the one from last year. He has come to look for her; he is all alone, the poor gentleman. So I have told him that you will go with him to keep him company."

Carlotta was looking at me with her beautiful brown eyes, and starting to smile, she murmured: "If he would like it, so would I."

How could I refuse? I declared: "But certainly I would also like it."

Then Mme Rondoli pushed her outside: "Go and dress quickly, quickly now, you will wear your blue dress and your hat the one with the flowers, hurry up."

As soon as her daughter had gone out she explained: "I still have two daughters but smaller. It is expensive you know to bring up four children; fortunately, at present, the eldest is out of the way."

Then she spoke to me of her life, of her husband, a railway employee who was no longer alive, and all the qualities of her second daughter, Carlotta.

The latter came back in, dressed in the same taste as the eldest, in an outfit which was both unusual and revealing.

Her mother inspected her from head to foot and judged her to be well to her liking. She said to us: "Be off now, my children."

Then, addressing her daughter: "Above all do not come back in this evening later than ten o'clock. You know that the door will be closed."

Carlotta replied: "Don't be afraid of anything, mother."

She took my arm and there I was, strolling with her through the streets like with her sister the year before.

I came back to the hotel for lunch; then I took my new girlfriend to Santa Margarita going on the same walk that I had had with Francesca.

And in the evening, although the door was due to be shut after ten o'clock, she did not return.

Then during the fifteen days I had at my disposal, I walked with Carlotta in the neighbourhood of Genoa. She never made me regret the other one.

I left her all in tears on the morning of my departure, leaving her with a souvenir, four bracelets for her mother.

And one of these days I count on returning to Italy, always dreaming with a certain anxiety mingled with hope that Mme Rondoli still possesses two daughters.

A PARISIAN ADVENTURE

Is there an instinct more acute than a woman's curiosity? Oh! To recognise, to experience, to touch what she has dreamed about! What wouldn't she do for that? When her restless curiosity is aroused, a woman will be very careless and commit every conceivable stupidity; she will have all the nerve and she will not retreat from anything. Of course, I am talking of real women, women endowed with this characteristic in triple measure, women who seem on the surface to be rational and level headed, but who have three secret hang-ups: first, typical female anxiety, always restless, second; craftiness tinged with good faith, that sort of craftiness of sanctimonious people who are both formidable and sophisticated and finally delightful malice, exquisite deceit, delicious treachery, in fact all those perverse qualities which drive some gullible imbecile lovers to suicide but enchant others.

When I mention 'adventure', I am referring to a little provincial lady, ordinary and honest – up till then. Her life apparently calm was spent in her household between a very busy husband and two children whom she brought up like a perfect wife. But her heart quivered with an insatiable curiosity, with an itch for the unknown. She thought of Paris ceaselessly and read the society newspapers avidly. The accounts of the parties, the clothes, the pleasures made her imagination boil over, but, above all, she was mysteriously stirred by articles full of innuendos, articles containing half-veiled allusions in clever phrases, which allowed her to glimpse distant horizons of guilty and consuming sexual delights.

From her position, she saw Paris as the apotheosis of magnificent and corrupt luxury.

Dreaming during the long nights, lulled by the regular snoring of her husband who slept at her side in a nightcap, she thought of those celebrated men whose names appeared on the front pages like big stars in a dark sky; she imagined their wild life, the continuous debauchery, the old fashioned and frightfully sumptuous orgies, with such intricate refinements of sensuality that she could hardly even contemplate them.

To her the Parisian streets seemed like chasms of human passions and all the houses were surely concealing the mysteries of unbridled sex.

She felt herself to be growing old. Indeed she was growing old without knowing anything of life apart from the regular drudgery, the hatefully monotonous and commonplace chores, which, they say, go to constitute happiness in the home. She was still attractive, preserved in that tranquil existence like preserved winter fruit in a closed cupboard, but, gnawed, ravaged and shrivelled by secret intense feelings. She wondered if she would die without having known all that tormenting exhilaration, without even being thrown once, just once, into that maelstrom of exquisite Parisian vice.

Eventually she made up her mind, got ready for a trip to Paris and invented an excuse. She arranged to be invited by her parents, and with her husband being unable to accompany her, she left alone.

As soon as she had arrived, she knew how to think up reasons why it would be necessary for her to be absent for a couple of days or rather a couple of nights, if need be, having rediscovered, she said, some friends who lived in the suburbs.

And so she searched. She roamed the boulevards seeing nothing apart from the registered and rootless prostitutes. She cast her eye over the grand cafés; read attentively the little adverts in the 'Figaro' which appeared each morning like a clarion call to love.

Nothing ever put her on the track of the big orgies of artistes and actresses; nothing led her to the temples of those debauches which like the cave of the 'Thousand and one nights' she imagined could only be opened with a magic word or like the cat-acombs in Rome where the mysteriesof a persecuted religion were secretly performed.

Her parents, who were petit-bourgeois, were not acquainted with any of those men she had in mind and whose names were buzzing in her head and in desperation she was thinking of returning home when luck came to her aid.

On one of the days, as she went down the 'Chaussée d'Antin' she stopped to look into a shop full of Japanese ornaments, which were so colourful that they seemed in a sort of way cheerful. She was examining the funny little ivory figurines, the strange bronzes, and the huge vases in brilliant enamel when she heard the proprietor talking at the back of the shop; with great deference he was showing to a little fat bald man with a beard an enormous pot-bellied dwarf, a unique piece, he was saying.

At each phrase uttered by the dealer, the name of the collector, a celebrated name, rang out like a trumpet. The other customers, young women and elegant gentlemen, were looking at the famous author with quick and furtive glances, which were strictly polite and respectful, while lovingly he was examining the porcelain dwarf. They were both as ugly as each other like two brothers from the same family.

The dealer was saying: "For you, Sir, Jean Varin, I will let it go for a thousand francs. It is exactly what it cost me. For anybody else it would be fifteen hundred francs. But I like to keep my artistic clients and I give them special prices. They all come to me, Monsieur Jean Varin. Yesterday Monsieur Busnach[1] bought a huge antique goblet. The other day I sold two candlesticks like that (you must admit, they are beautiful) to Alexander Dumas[2]. That piece you have in your hand now, if Monsieur Zola[3] saw it, it would be sold, Monsieur Varin."

The author was very perplexed and undecided; he was attracted by the object, but he was thinking about the price and he was oblivious to the looks he was receiving to such an extent that he might well have been alone in the desert.

She had gone in, trembling and she was looking straight at him shamelessly; she was not even asking herself whether he was handsome, elegant or young. It was Jean Varin, himself, the Jean Varin!

After much hesitation and a painful struggle, he replaced the vase on the table: "No", he said. "It is too expensive."

The dealer became even more eloquent: "Oh! Monsieur Jean Varin, too expensive? This is worth two thousand francs if it is worth a sou."

The literary man looked at the chap with the enamel eyes and sadly replied: "I agree but he is too dear for me."

Then, she, overcome with crazy effrontery, came forward and said: "For me, how much for this fellow?"

The dealer, taken aback, replied:

"Fifteen hundred francs, Madame."

"I'll take it."

The author, who until that moment had not even noticed her, turned round abruptly; he looked her up and down observing her through half closed eyes; then, as an expert, he scrutinised her.

She was charming, animated and suddenly fired up by that flame which until then had been dormant. And then for a woman who buys an ornament for fifteen hundred francs, it can't have been the first visit.

Then she made a movement of delightful sensitivity and turning towards him with a quavering voice: "Pardon, sir, without a doubt, I have been a little quick; perhaps you have not said your last word."

He bowed: "I have said it Madame."

But, she, quite flustered: "Well, at least, sir, today or later, if you happen to change your mind, this ornament is yours. I only bought it because you liked it."

He smiled, visibly flattered and said: "So, how do you know me?"

So she told him at her admiration, quoted from his writing, and spoke eloquently.

To continue the conversation, he leant on a piece of furniture with his elbows; he fixed her with his penetrating gaze and tried to fathom her out.

The dealer, happy to have this living advertisement for some new customers who had come in, shouted at once from the back of the shop: "Well, look at that, Monsieur Jean Varin. Isn't it beautiful?" Then all heads were turned and she quivered with pleasure to be chatting like this intimately with a famous person.

Finally, intoxicated, like a general who gives the order for the attack, she had the supreme effrontery. She said: "Sir, give me the great pleasure, the very great pleasure. Allow me to offer you this chap as a souvenir from a woman who admires you passionately and whom you have only seen for ten minutes."

He refused. She insisted. Very amused and laughing heartily, he resisted.

Obstinately, she told him: "Oh, well! I am going to take him to your home straightaway. Where do you live?"

He refused to give his address, but she had already got it from the dealer and having paid for her acquisition, she rushed out for a cab. The author ran to catch her because he did not wish to be liable for the gift when he did not know to whom to return it. In his panic to join her he practically fell on top of her, having been knocked over by the jolt of the cab which had already started on its journey. Then he sat down at her side extremely annoyed.

It was no good begging and insisting. She proved intractable. As they came up to the door, she set out her conditions. She said: "I will consent not to leave you with this object; if to-day you will carry out all my wishes."

The idea seemed to him to be so laughable that he accepted.

She asked: "What do you normally do at this hour?"

After a slight hesitation, he said: "I go for a walk."

So in a firm voice, she commanded: "To the 'Bois de Boulogne."

They set off.

He was required to name for her all the well-known women, especially the immoral ones, with intimate details about them, their life, their habits, their homes, their vices.

Night fell. "What do you do every day at this hour?" she said.

Laughing, he replied: "I have an absinthe."

Then seriously she added: "Very well, sir, let us have an absinthe."

They went into a large boulevard café which he frequented, and where he met some colleagues. He introduced them all to her. She was mad with joy and these words went round and round in her head: "At last. At last!"

The time went by and she asked: "Is it time for your dinner?"

He replied, "Yes, Madame."

Well, sir, let us go and have dinner."

While leaving the Café Bignon, she said: "In the evenings that do you do?"

He looked at her intently: "That all depends; sometimes I go to the theatre."

They went to the Vaudeville; as a favour and thanks to him, it was the supreme triumph; they were seated together on the armchairs in the circle; she was seen by the whole audience.

The show over, he kissed her hand gallantly: "It remains for me, Madame, to thank you for a delightful day."

She interrupted him: "At this hour, what do you do every night?"

"But …..but ….. I return home."

She started to laugh – nervously.

"Very well, sir, lets go to your home."

And they did not speak any more. At times she was shaking and trembling from head to foot; she had both the urge to flee and the urge to stay, but at the bottom of her heart a very firm resolve to go right to the end.

On the stairs her emotion was becoming so acute that she clung to the banisters; he went up in front, panting, a candle in his hand.

As soon as she was in the bedroom, she got undressed very quickly and slipped into the bed without saying a word; and she waited huddled against the wall. But she was simple as only the legitimate wife of a country solicitor can be and he was more demanding than a pasha with three tails. They did not relate to one another, not at all.

The night went by only disturbed by the ticking of the clock and, motionless, she thought of her conjugal nights; and under the yellow rays of a Chinese lantern, sad and upset, she looked at this little man lying on his back at her side with his rounded belly lifting the sheet like a gas balloon. He was snoring like an organ pipe, with prolonged snorts and comic choking sounds. His twenty hairs, tired of their fixed position concealing the devastation of his baldness, profited from his rest and stood up oddly. A thread of saliva trickled from a corner of his half open mouth.

At last the dawn came and a little light filtered through the drawn curtains. She got up and dressed without a sound and as she half opened the door, she made the lock squeak and he awoke, rubbing his eyes.

It was several seconds before he completely recovered his senses; then, when the adventure came back to him, he asked: "Oh, well, you are leaving?"

Confused, she remained standing and stammered: "Why, yes, it is morning."

He sat up. "Look", he said, "it is now my turn to ask you something."

She did not reply and he went on: "Since yesterday, you have jolly well surprised me. Be frank, admit to me why you did all that because I don't understand a thing?"

She came closer quietly, blushing: "I wanted to know …. about vice …. the dissolute life ….ah well …. ah well …. it is not enjoyable."

Then she rushed out, went down the stairs and flung herself into the street.

An army of street cleaners were sweeping up. They were sweeping the pavements and the cobblestones, pushing all the rubbish into the gutter. With the same regular movements, like mowers in the meadows, they pushed the dirt in front of them, street after street, like mechanical puppets mowing automatically with the same spring.

And it seemed to her that they had just swept something from her, and pushed into the gutter and into the drains her overexcited dreams.

She returned home, breathless and frozen; the only thing in her head was the image of the movement of the brooms cleaning Paris in the morning.

And as soon as she was in her bedroom, she sobbed.

THE LOG

The drawing room was small, discreetly scented and with thick wallpaper. In a wide fireplace a big fire was blazing. A single lamp resting on the corner of the mantelpiece with a shade of old fashioned lace threw a soft light on the two people who were chatting.

She was an old lady with white hair, the mistress of the house, one of those adorable old people whose skin had no wrinkles and was smooth like fine paper; she was heavily scented, quite impregnated with perfumes, with those delicate essences with which she had bathed her skin for so long a time; when you kissed her hand you were reminded of the odour which hits you when you open a box of Florentine iris powder.

He was a very old and very close friend, unmarried, a travelling companion in life. Nothing more, needless to say.

They had stopped conversing for about a minute, and they were both looking at the fire, dreaming of no matter what; it was one of those silences, very dear to people who have no need to be always talking to please one another.

Suddenly a big log, a tree stump spiked with flaming roots, collapsed. It jumped over the firedogs, shot into the room and rolled on to the carpet, throwing flaming sparks all round her.

The little lady with a little cry stood up ready to escape, while he, with blows from his boot kicked the flaming lump back into the huge fireplace and stamped out the burning embers spread round about.

After the crisis was over, there was still a strong smell of burning in the air. He sat down again opposite her and smiled:

"There you see", he said, pointing to the log replaced in the grate; "there you see why I was never married".

She looked at him, astonished, with the inquisitive gaze of a woman who wishes to know, the eye of a woman who is no longer young, whose curiosity is thoughtful, tortuous and often mischievous.

She asked: "How did that happen?"

He replied: "Oh! It is quite a story, sad enough and nasty."

My old comrades were often astonished at the coolness which suddenly sprang up between me and one of my best friends – his first name was Julian. They did not understand how two close friends, two inseparables – which we were – could all of a sudden become almost strangers to one another. But here is the secret of our parting.

In the past, he and I used to live together. We were never parted and the friendship which bound us seemed so strong that nothing should have been able to break it.

One evening he came in and announced to me his forthcoming marriage.

I received a blow to my heart as if he had robbed me or betrayed me. When a friend gets married it is finished, really finished. The jealous affection of a woman, that peevish, anxious and physical affection does not tolerate the vigorous and frank attachment of mind, heart and confidence which exists between two men. You see, my dear, whatever might be the nature of the love which binds them together, the man and the woman are always different in thought and intellect; they exist as two belligerents; they are from a race apart; there always has to be a tamer and a tamed, a master and a slave; sometimes one, sometimes the other; they are never two equals. The hands may be held, hands tingling with passion; they are never clasped with a firm and loyal pressure, which opens hearts and lays them bare in a surge of strong, sincere and manly affection. Sensible people, instead of marrying and procreating children as consolation for their advanced years, children who will abandon them, should seek a good and solid friend and grow old with him enjoying that harmony of thinking that can only exist between two men.

Finally my friend Julian got married; she was pretty, his wife, and charming, a little blonde with curly hair, lively and curvaceous; she seemed to adore him.

At first I did not go to their house much, afraid of upsetting their loving relationship and feeling that I would be too much in the way. Yet they appeared to call me incessantly, to ask me round and to like me.

Little by little I allowed myself to be seduced by the gentle charm of their married life and I frequently used to dine with them; but often back home at night, I thought of doing like him and getting married; I was now finding my empty house really sad.

As for them they doted on each other and were never parted. Then, one evening, Julian dropped me a note, inviting me to come to dinner and I went. "My good chap", he said, "it is going to be necessary for me to be absent after dinner for some business. I will not be back before eleven o'clock but at eleven precisely I will return. I am relying on you to keep Berthe company."

The young woman was smiling: "Besides, it was me who had the idea to send for you," she said.

I shook her hand: "You are very kind". And I felt on my fingers a prolonged and friendly pressure. I was not on my guard. We sat down at table and at eight o'clock Julian left us.

As soon as he had left, a sort of peculiar embarrassment sprang up abruptly between his wife and me. We had never found ourselves alone before, and despite our intimacy which was growing each day, the tête-à-tête placed us in a new situation. At first, to fill embarrassing silences, I spoke of vague and trifling matters; she never responded and stayed facing me on the other side of the fireplace; her head was lowered and her feet were stretched out to the fire; she had an indecisive look as if lost in deep thoughts. When I had exhausted banal topics, I fell silent. It is astonishing how sometimes it is not easy to find things to say. Then I felt something in the air, something invisible a 'je ne sais quoi' impossible to express, that mysterious signal in

41

your direction that warns you of hidden intentions, good or bad, from another person.

The painful silence lasted some time. Then Berthe said to me: "Put a log on the fire, my friend, you can see that it is going to go out." I opened the log basket – situated just like yours – and I took out the biggest log which I placed as in a pyramid on top of the other pieces of wood which were three-quarters consumed.

Then the silence began again.

After few minutes, the log blazed in such a way that it was scorching our faces. The young woman looked up to me; her eyes seemed strange. "Now it is too hot," she said, "so let's go and sit on the sofa."

Then suddenly, looking me straight in the face, she said: "what do you do if a woman told you that she loved you?"

Completely taken aback, I replied: "Good God, the case has never arisen, and then, that would depend on the woman."

She started to laugh, with a nervous, shrill laugh, one of those forced laughs which could have easily broken a wineglass and she added:

"Men are never daring nor subtle." She was silent and then went on:

"Paul, have you sometimes been in love?"

I admitted it: "Yes, I have been in love."

"Tell me about it," she said.

I told her an ordinary sort of story. She listened attentively with frequent signs of scorn and disapproval, and, suddenly: "No, you don't understand anything. In my opinion for love to be right, it needs to shatter the heart, strain the nerves and split the head; it needs – how shall I put it? – to be dangerous, even terrifying, almost criminal, practically sacrilegious, a sort of treason. I mean that it needs to break with hallowed conventions, with laws, with fraternal ties; when love is calm, easy, legal and without risk, is it really love?"

I no longer knew what to reply, and silently I contented myself with this philosophical exclamation: Oh! The female brain, there you have it!

While talking, she had put on a different, innocent air. Then, lying down, she stretched herself out with her head on my shoulder; her dress was a little revealing and showed a glimpse of a red silk stocking, which was at times lit up by flickers from the hearth.

After a minute she said: "I am frightening you." I protested. Without looking at me she leant right up against my chest and said: "If I told you that I loved you, what would you do?" And before I could find a reply, her arms were round my neck, pulling my head quickly towards her and her lips were joining mine.

Ah! My dear friend, I was not amused, I am telling you! What! Deceive Julian? Become the lover of this cunning and perverted little fool, frightfully sexy no doubt but for whom her husband was no longer enough! Incessantly to betray and deceive a friend, to play with love for the sole attraction of a forbidden fruit, of a danger defied and the risk of a friendship ruined! No. That was hardly me. But what to do? Play the innocent! Very stupid and moreover a very difficult part, for this girl was frightening in her disloyalty, fired up with daring, impulsive and passionate. Oh! I wish I had never felt from her mouth the penetrating kiss of a woman ready to give herself, to throw me the first stone ……..

……….Indeed, one minute more ….. you do understand, don't you? One minute more and …. I was …. no, she was…. Sorry, it was or rather I would have been it, when, look, a terrible noise made us both jump.

The log, Madame, yes the log was launching itself into the room, knocking over the tongs and the fireguard, rolling like a fireball, setting light to the carpet and ending up under an armchairwhich would have inevitably caught fire.

I rushed for it like a madman, and while I was pushing this saviour firebrand back into the grate, suddenly the door opened! Julian, all cheerful, came in. He cried: "I am free, the business was finished two hours early!"

Yes, my friend, I would have been caught red-handed; and here you see the consequences!

So I have made sure never to be caught again in a similar situation, never, never. After that I saw that Julian was giving me the cold shoulder, as one says. Obviously his wife was undermining our friendship and little by little he put me off from visiting his house and now we have stopped seeing each other.

I have never got married. That must no longer astonish you.

MOONLIGHT

Mme Julie Roubère was expecting her elder sister, Mme Henriette Letoré who was coming back from a trip to Switzerland.

The Letoré household had departed nearly six weeks ago. Henriette had let her husband return alone to their property in Calvados, where business interests had summoned him, and she was coming to spend a few days with her sister in Paris…

The evening was falling. The small drawing room, in the fading light, Mme Roubère was reading absentmindedly, her eyes looking up at every sound.

At last the bell rang and her sister appeared, completely enveloped in her heavy travelling clothes. Straightaway they hugged each other violently, stopping to kiss and then instantly to embrace again.

Next they spoke, questioning each other on their health, their families and thousand other things, chattering with hurried half-finished sentences, skipping from one word to another, while Henriette unfastened her veil and her hat.

Night had fallen. Mme Roubère rang for a lamp and as soon as the light had arrived, she looked at her sister ready to kiss her again. But alarmed, she stopped in her tracks without speaking. On her temples Mme Leloré had two big locks of white hair. All the rest of her head was dark black and gleaming; but there all on their own those two silvery streaks stretched back from both sides to lose themselves in the dark mass of her hair. Yet she was scarcely twenty-four and that had come about suddenly since her departure for Switzerland. Rooted to the spot Mme Roubère looked at her in amazement, ready to weep as if some mysterious and terrible misfortune had befallen her sister; and she asked:

"What is it, Henriette?"

With a sad and sickly smile, the other replied:

"But it's nothing, I assure you. You are looking at my white hair?"

But Mme Roubère seized her impetuously by the shoulders, and, giving her a searching glance, she repeated:

"What is it? Tell me what happened and if you are lying, I can easily tell."

They stayed facing one another, and Henriette who was becoming pale enough to faint, had tears in the corners of her downcast eyes.

Her sister repeated:

"What has happened to you?" What is it? Answer me?"

Then, in a defeated voice, the other muttered:

"I have ….. I have a lover."

And throwing her head on the shoulder of her young sister, she sobbed.

Next after she had calmed down a little and the thumping of her chest had subsided, she suddenly started to speak, as if to let out that secret and to release that pain to a kindred soul.

Then holding hands tightly, the two women sank down on a sofa at the back of the darkened drawing room and the youngest putting her arms round the neck of the eldest and holding her close to her heart, listened.

*

Oh! I admit I have no excuse. I don't understand it myself and since that day I have been crazy. Take care, little sister, look out yourself; if you knew how weak we are, how we yield, how quickly we fall! It takes nothing, so little, so very little, an emotion, one of those sudden moods which pass through our mind, one of those inclinations we all have at certain moments, to open our arms, to cherish and to embrace.

You are acquainted with my husband and you know how I love him; but he is mature and rational and understands nothing of the tender vibrations of a woman's heart. He is always, always the same, always nice, always smiling, always obliging, always perfect. Oh! How I wish sometimes that he might seize me in his arms abruptly, that he might embrace me with those lingering and sweet kisses which unite two beings, which are like silent confidences; how I wish that he might have some relaxed attitudes, some weaknesses, some need of me, my caresses and my tears.

All that is stupid; but we are like that, some of us. What can we do?

And yet the thought of deceiving him has never crossed my mind. To-day it is done, without love, without reason, with nothing; all because there was a moon one night on lake Lucerne.

During the month we travelled together, my husband with his calm indifference paralysed my enthusiasm and extinguished my excitement. When we used to descend the hillsides at sunrise in the coach with its four horses at the gallop, and when we used to see in the light morning mist the long valleys, the woods, the rivers, the villages, I used to clap my hands in delight, saying to him: "How beautiful it is, my dear, so give me a kiss!" He used to reply with a frigid and benevolent smile and shrugging his shoulders slightly: "The fact that the countryside pleases you is no reason for us to embrace one another."

And that froze me to the heart. Yet it seems to me that when we love one another, we must always have the urge to love still more in front of sights which move us.

In the end I had the bubbling of romance inside me and he was preventing it from being displayed. I was a little like a boiler full of steam and hermetically sealed.

One evening (we had been staying in a hotel at Fluelen for four days), Robert suffering from a slight migraine went to bed straight after dinner and I went for a walk all alone by the side of the lake.

It was a fairy tale night. In the middle of the sky there was a full moon; the huge snow covered mountains appeared to be capped with silver and the water was ruffled with little glinting ripples. The air was sweet with that penetrating mildness which makes us limp and ready to swoon, touched for no reason. But how the soul is sensitive and vibrant at such moments! How quickly it twitches and how inevitably it feels the effects!

I sat down on the grass and watched that gloomy and bewitching lake; and something strange happened to me. An insatiable need for love came over me, a rebellion against the dull platitudes of my life. What, so, would I never be in the arms of a loved one beside a lake bathed by the moon? Would I never feel raining down on me those deep, delicious and disturbing kisses during those sweet nights which seem to have been made in heaven for tender affection? Would I never be feverishly embraced by frantic arms in the pale shadow of a summer's night?

Then I started to cry like a mad thing.

I heard a noise behind me. A man was standing looking at me. When I turned round, he recognised me and approached: "You are crying, Madame?"

It was a young lawyer who was travelling with his mother, and we had met several times. His eyes had often followed me.

I was so upset that I did not know what to reply, what to think. I got up and said that I was unwell.

He began to walk beside me in a natural and respectful manner and he conversed with me about our travels. Everything that I had felt found its expression in him. He understood everything which gave me a thrill – just like me, better than me. Suddenly he recited some verse, some of Musset's[1] poems. I choked with indescribable emotion. It seemed to me that the mountains themselves, the lake and the moonlight were singing things which were unutterably sweet…...

And all that, I don't know how and why, resulted in a sort of hallucination…...

As for him ….. I only saw him again the next day when he was leaving.

He gave me his card!.....

*

And Mme Letoré, swooning in the arms of her sister, let out groans, almost screams.

Then Mme Roubère, reverentially and gravely, quite gently declared:

"You see, big sister, very often it is not a man whom we love, but love itself. And on that evening then, it was the moonlight which was your true lover."

A PASSION

The sea was calm and sparkling, hardly stirred by the tide. The whole town of Le Havre was on the pier watching the ships entering.

They could be seen in the distance, lots of them, some – large steamers smothered with smoke, the others – sailing ships being towed by almost invisible tugs, their bare masts sticking up into the sky like trees without foliage.

They came from all quarters of the horizon, running in towards the narrow harbour entrance which was swallowing these monsters; and they groaned, they squealed and they whistled spitting out jets of steam like whales blowing.

Two young officers were walking on the crowded mole, saluting and being saluted, sometimes stopping to chat.

Suddenly one of them, the tallest, Paul d'Henricel grabbed the arm of his comrade, Jean Renoldi and said in a low voice: "Look, here comes Mme Poinçot; watch, I'm sure that she has her eye on you."

She was coming on the arm of her husband, a rich ship-owner. She was a woman of about forty, still very attractive, a little large, but thanks to the charm of her stout figure, well preserved like a twenty year old... Among her friends she was called the Goddess on account of her proud bearing, her large dark eyes, and the total nobility of her person. She had remained irreproachable and never had a suspicion blemished her life. She was quoted as an example of a woman so honourable and unpretentious that no man had dared to have second thoughts in her direction.

But there it was, for a month now, Paul d'Henricel was swearing to his friend Renoldi that Mme Poinçet was soft on him; and he insisted: "Be sure I am not mistaken; I see it clearly; she loves you, she loves you passionately like a chaste woman who has never been in love. Forty years is a terrible age for honest women when they have some sensuality; they become crazy and do mad things. She is touched, my good chap, that one; like a wounded bird she is falling, she is going to fall into your arms…... Look, watch."

The tall woman, preceded by her two daughters aged twelve and fifteen, was approaching and suddenly turned pale when she saw the officer. With a fixed gaze she was looking at him ardently and seemed to be aware of nothing else around her, neither her children, nor her husband, nor the crowd. She acknowledged the greeting of some young people without turning her face which lit up with such a flame that a doubt finally sank into the mind of lieutenant Renoldi.

His friend murmured: "I was sure of it, have you seen it this time? Gosh, she is still a rich picking."

But Jean Renoldi was not wanting a society affair. Not really looking for love, above all he desired a quiet life and was content with the occasional liaisons which a young man always encounters. All the accompanying sentimentality, the attentions, the tender feelings required by a well educated woman bored him. The strings, light as they might be, which always became tangled up in an affair of this sort, frightened him. He used to say: "At the end of a month I have had enough of it and out of politeness I am obliged to hang around for six months." Then, the break-up, the scenes, the allusions, the woman dropped, clinging on, exasperated him.

He avoided meeting Mme Poinçot.

But one evening, he found himself next to her at table during a dinner; unceasingly he had the passionate stare of his neighbour on his face, in his eye, right into his soul; their hands touched and almost involuntarily they were clasped together. Already it was the beginning of a liaison.

He saw her again, always in spite of himself; he softened overcome by a sort of conceited pity for the violent passion of this woman. So he allowed himself to be loved while he had the feeling of gallantry really hoping that it would stay that way.

But one day she gave him a date, to see him and to chat freely, so she said. She fell swooning into his arms; and he was really forced to be her lover.

That lasted six months. She adored him with an unbridled, breathtaking love. Imprisoned by this fanatical passion she thought of nothing else; she gave everything, her body, her soul, her reputation, her position, her happiness, she threw it all away into this flame in her heart, like one throws all ones precious possessions on to a bonfire to sacrifice them.

As for him, for a long time he had had enough of it and was bitterly regretting the easy conquests of a handsome officer. But he was bound, held captive. At every opportunity she used to tell him: "I have given you everything; what more do you want?" He really felt like replying: "But I have asked you for nothing, and please take back what you have given me." Without caring whether she was seen, compromised, lost, she came to his quarters each evening, always more passionate. She launched herself into his arms and hugged him, swooning with elated kisses which annoyed him horribly. He used to say in a bored voice: "Come on, be reasonable." She replied: "I love you; and she fell down on her knees, to gaze at him attentively for a long time in a posture of adoration. Under that obsessed look, finally he became exasperated and wanted to lift her up: "Come on, sit down, let's talk." She murmured: "No, let me be," and she stayed there her soul in ecstasy.

He said to his friend d'Henricel: "You know. I will thump her. I do not want it any more, I don't want it any more. It must end; and straightaway!" Then he added: "What do you advise me to do?" The other replied: "Break with her." But Renoldi continued, shrugging his shoulders: "You speak of it without being involved, you think it is easy to break with a woman who torments you with attentions, who tortures you with kindness, who persecutes you with her affection, a woman whose sole concern is to please you and whose unique fault is to give herself to you in spite of yourself."

But, as it happened, one morning it was learnt that the regiment was going to move; Renoldi began to dance with joy. He was saved! Saved without scenes, without cries! Saved! ….. It was no more than being patient for a couple of months! ….. Saved! …..

She came to see him in the evening, even more fanatical than normal. She had heard the terrible news and without removing her hat she took his hands, clasped them nervously, and looking at him straight in the eye in a vibrant determined voice she said: "You are going to leave, I know it. At first I was broken hearted. Then I realised what I had to do. I no longer hesitated. I am coming to give you the greatest proof of my love that a woman can offer: I am following you. For you I am abandoning my husband, my children, my family. I am lost, but I am happy. I feel that I am giving myself to you anew. It is the last and greatest sacrifice. I am yours for ever!"

A cold sweat ran down his back; he was seized by dumb and furious rage, with impotent anger. However he calmed down and in a disinterested and mild tone of voice, refused her sacrifice, attempted to appease her, to reason with her and to make her face up to her folly! With her dark eyes and scornful lip, she listened to him without replying. When he had finished, she said to him simply: "Are you going to be a coward? Would you be one of those types who seduce a woman, then abandon her at the first whim?"

He turned pale and started to reason with her again. He pointed out the inevitable consequence of such an action right until death – their life ruined; shunned by society…… Stubbornly she replied: "What does it matter when one is in love!"

Then suddenly he burst out: "All right! No. I don't want it. Do you hear? I don't want it, I forbid you." Then carried away with his long resentment, he emptied his heart: "Ah! To hell with you. Seeing that you have loved me long enough in spite of me, it would be the last straw to take you away with me. No thanks, honestly!"

She did not reply but her livid face had become gradually and painfully tense as if all her nerves and muscles were being twisted. And she went off without saying goodbye.

That very night she took an overdose. For eight days she was thought to be at death's door. And in the town there was talk; she was pitied and her fault was excused thanks to the violence of her passion; for extreme feelings are always forgiven, even when reprehensible, if they are heroically expressed. A woman who kills herself has, so to speak, no longer committed adultery. And soon there was a sort of general disapproval, a unanimous impression of blame against lieutenant Renoldi who was refusing to see her again.

It was spread about that he had abandoned her, betrayed her and beaten her. The colonel overcome with pity discreetly alluded to the matter and had a word with his officer. Paul d'Henricel went to find his friend: "Oh! For heaven's sake, my good chap, one doesn't let a woman die; it is not decent that."

The other, exasperated, told his friend who had made a slanderous statement, to be silent. They fought each other. Renoldi, to the general satisfaction, was wounded and was laid up in bed a long time.

She knew about it and loved him more for it, believing that he had fought for her; but unable to leave the room she did not see him again before the departure of the regiment.

He had been three months at Lille when one morning he received a visit from a young woman, the sister of his former mistress.

After a long illness and a despair which she was unable to overcome, Mme Poinçot was going to die. She was a hopeless case. She wished to see him for a minute, no more than a minute before closing her eyes for ever.

The absence and time had appeased the young man's anger and disgust. He was touched, he wept and left for Le Havre.

She appeared to be dying. They were left alone and on the deathbed of the woman he had killed in spite of himself he had a crisis of dreadful grief. He sobbed and with gentle and loving lips; he kissed her in a way he had never done. He stammered: "No, no, you will not die, you will be cured, we will love each other ….. we will love each other ….. always…."

She murmured: "Is it true? You love me?" And in his sorrow he swore it and promised to wait for her when she was better. Then while kissing the very wasted hands of the poor woman whose heart was beating irregularly, he grieved over her for a long time.

The next day he returned to his garrison.

Six weeks later she rejoined him, quite aged, barely recognisable, and still more enamoured.

Deeply moved he took her back. Then since they were living together as man and wife, the very same colonel who was indignant when he abandoned her now protested against this illegitimate situation, incompatible with the good example which officers should set in a regiment. He warned his subordinate, then he put his foor down and Renoldi handed in his resignation.

They went to live in a villa on the edge of the Mediterranean the classic sea for the amorous.

Three years rolled by. Renoldi, submitting to the yoke, was defeated and became used to that persevering affection. She now had white hair.

He considered himself as a man finished, drowned. Every ambition, every career, every achievement, every joy was now for him forbidden.

Then one morning, a card was brought in: 'Joseph Poinçot, ship-owner Le Havre.' The husband! The husband who had said nothing accepting that one does not struggle against the hopeless obstinacy of women. What did he want?

He was waiting in the garden, having declined to enter the villa. He saluted politely and did not want to sit down even on a bench on a path. He began to speak slowly and clearly:

"Sir, I have not come to reproach you; I know only too well how these things happen. I have suffered …. We have suffered ….. A sort of … of …of… destiny. I would never have disturbed you in your retirement if the situation had not changed. I have two daughters, sir. One of them, the eldest, loves a young man and is loved by him. But the family of this boy opposes the marriage, objecting to the situation of the ….. mother of my daughter. I have neither anger nor resentment but, sir, I adore my children. Therefore I have come to ask you to give me back my ….. wife; I hope that to-day she will consent to come home ….. to her home. As for me, I will make it appear that I have forgotten for ….. for the sake of my daughters."

Renoldi felt his heart giving a violent beat and a delirium of joy flooded over him, like a condemned man who receives a pardon.

He stammered: "But yes ….. certainly, sir ….. I myself … believe me ….. without a doubt ….. it is right, too right."

And he felt like taking the hands of this man, clasping him in his arms and kissing him on both cheeks.

He continued: "So do come in. You will be better in the drawing room; I am going to fetch her."

This time M. Poinçot resisted no longer and he sat down.

Renoldi bounded up the stairs; then outside the door of his mistress he steadied himself and entered solemnly: "Someone is asking for you downstairs," he said; "it is a communication concerning your daughters." She stood up: "My daughters? What? So what is it? They are not dead?"

He replied: "No. But there is a serious problem which only you can sort out."

She did not listen any more and went rapidly downstairs.

He slumped down on to a chair, quite flustered, and waited.

He waited a long time, a long time. Then as two irritated voices floated up to him across the ceiling, he made the decision to go down.

Mme Poinçot was standing up, exasperated, prepared to leave while her husband was holding her back, clutching her dress and repeating: "But, so you realise that you are losing our daughters, your daughters, our children!"

Stubbornly she was replying: "I will not go back home with you." Renoldi understood completely, he approached, tottering, and stammered: "What? She is refusing?" She turned round towards him and as a result of a kind of modesty in the presence of her legal husband, she no longer used the familiar form of address: "Do you know what he is asking? He wants me to return to live under his roof!" She was snarling with immense contempt for this man who was imploring her practically on his knees.

Then Renoldi, with the determination of a man who is plying his last card, started to speak in his turn, to plead the cause of the poor girls, the cause of the husband, his cause. And when he paused, searching for some new argument, M. Poinçot, at the end of his tether and instinctively out of habit resorting to his old familiar tone: "Look, Delphine, think of your daughters."

Then she enveloped the two of them with a look of supreme scorn and escaping with a rush towards the stairs, she yelled at them: "You are both miserable wretches!"

Left on their own, they looked at each other for a moment distressed and totally demoralised; M. Poinçot picked up his hat which had fallen down beside him, dusted his knees whitened by the floor with his hand, then as Renoldi was conducting him towards the door, with a despairing gesture while saying goodbye: "We are really unfortunate, sir."

Then he went off with a heavy step.

AT THE BEDSIDE

A big fire was blazing in the grate. On the Japanese table two teacups were facing each other while the teapot was steaming beside the sugar bowl which was flanked by a decanter of rum.

The count de Sallure threw his hat, his gloves and his fur coat on to a chair, while the countess, having escaped from her exit at the ball, adjusted her hair a little in front of the mirror. She was smiling quietly to herself and with the tips of her slender fingers gleaming with rings, she patted her curls on her temples.Then she turned towards her husband. He had been watching her for some seconds and seemed to be hesitating as if embarrassed by a private thought.

Finally he said:

"You made quite a hit this evening?"

She looked him in the eye, her face lit up with a flicker of triumph and defiance. She replied:

"I was very much hoping to!"

Then she sat down on her chair. He positioned himself facing her and, taking a brioche, he replied:

"It was pretty ridiculous ….. for me!"

She asked:

"Is there going to be a scene? Do you intend to criticise me?"

"No, my dear, I am only saying that M. Burel was almost improper towards you. If ….. if ….. I had my rights ….. I would be angry."

"My dear, be frank. You no longer think today like you used to think last year, that's all. When I knew that you had a mistress, a mistress whom you love, it is hardly your business if people court me or not. I told you that I was upset, like you told me this evening but with more justification; my friend, you compromise Mme de Servy, you make trouble for me and make me ridiculous. What did you reply? Oh! You have let me understand perfectly that I was free, that marriage between intelligent people was only an association of interests, a social tie but not a moral one. Is it true? You have made me aware that your mistress was infinitely better than me, more seductive, more of a woman! You said: more of a woman. All that was shrouded with the respect belonging to a well educated man, dressed up with compliments and pronounced with a delicacy to which I pay tribute. But none the less I have understood perfectly.

It has been agreed that from now on we will live together but completely separated. We have a child which forms a bond of union between us.

You have practically let me guess that you were only keeping up appearances that I could, if I wished, take a lover provided that the liaison remains secret. You have expounded at length and very well on the sensitivity of women and on their skill at handling the conventions etc.

I have understood, my friend, understood perfectly. So you were in love, very much in love with Mme de Servy, and my legitimate affection, my legal affection embarrassed you. Doubtless I spend some of your means. Since then we have lived apart. We go out in society together, we come back together but then we go our separate ways.

But, now for a month or two, you have taken the attitude of a jealous man. What does that mean?"

"My dear, I am not at all jealous but I am afraid to see you compromised. You are young, lively and adventurous."

"Sorry, if we are talking of adventures, all I am asking is that things should be even between us."

"Look, please do not joke. I am speaking to you as a friend. As for everything you have just said, it is greatly exaggerated."

"Not at all. You have admitted it; you have confessed your affair to me, which is equivalent to giving me an authorisation to follow your example. I have not done so........."

"Excuse me........."

"Will you let me finish. I have not done it. I do not have a lover and I have not had one ..... up to now. I am waiting ..... I am looking ..... I have not found one. I need someone good .... Better than you..... It is a compliment that I am giving you and you do not seem to have noticed it."

"My dear, all these jokes are completely out of place."

"But I am not joking in the least. You have spoken to me about the eighteenth century, you have given me to understand that you were Regency. I have forgotten nothing. The day when it will suit me to stop being what I am, will not matter to you, do you hear, without a shadow of doubt you will be a cuckold like the others."

"Oh! Can you pronounce the same words?"

"The same words! ..... But you laughed like mad when Mme de Gers declared that M. de Servy had the air of a cuckold in search of his horns."

"What may seem funny in the mouth of Mme de Gers becomes improper in yours."

"Not at all. You find the word – cuckold – very amusing when it is a question of M. de Servy and you consider it to be very vulgar when it refers to you. Besides I don't hold with that expression. I only uttered it to see if you were ready."

"Ready ..... for what?"

"To be it. When a man gets annoyed hearing this word spoken, it is that he is getting ..... impatient. In two months you will be the first to joke if I speak of ..... a bit of luck. Then ..... yes ..... when you are it, you don't realise it."

"This evening you have really lost your manners. I've never seen you like this."

"Ah! Look ..... I have changed ..... for the worse. It is your fault."

"Look, my dear, let us speak seriously, please, I beg you not to accept, like you have done this evening, the unseemly advances of M. Burel."

"You are jealous. I was right."

"But no, not at all. I simply do not wish to be a subject of ridicule. I do not like ridicule. And if I see that gentleman talking to you again ….. examining your shoulders ….. or rather your bosom….."

"He was looking for a megaphone."

"I ….. will box his ears."

"Are you, by any chance, becoming amorous for me?"

"I might be with a woman less attractive"

"Oh! There you go! As for me, I am no longer amorous for you!"

The count got up. He went round the little table and going behind her he planted a quick kiss on her neck. She stood up with a shock, and looking him straight in the eye: "No more jokes like that, if you please. We are living apart. It is finished."

"Look, don't get annoyed. I've been finding you ravishing for some time."

"Then ….. then ….. it is I who have won. You find me ….. ready ….. as well."

"My dear, I find you ravishing, your arms, your shoulders, your complexion."

"Which attracted M. Burel….."

"You are cruel….. But, there ….. true ….. I do not know a woman as seductive as you."

"You have been fasting."

"What?"

"I said: you have been fasting."

"How so?"

"When one is fasting, one is hungry and when one is hungry, one decides to eat things which at another time one would not like. I am the dish ….. in the past neglected ---- this evening … you would not mind having a taste…."

"Oh! Marguerite! Who has taught you to say things like that?"

"You! Let's see: Since your break up with Mme de Servy, you've had, to my knowledge, four mistresses, women on the loose, dancers by profession."

"I will be brutally frank and I won't beat about the bush. I have again become amorous for you. To tell the truth, very much so. So there you are."

"Hold on, hold on. So you would like ….. to begin again?"

"Yes, Madame."

"This evening!"

"Oh! Marguerite!"

"Good. There you see you are shocked again. My dear, let us consider… There is nothing between us any more, right? I am your wife, it is true but your wife, a free woman. I am going to make a commitment in another sense, you are asking me a favour. I will grant it to you ….. at an equivalent price."

"I don't understand."

"Let me explain. Am I as good as your trollops? Be frank."

"A thousand times better."

"Better than the best."

"A thousand times."

"Well, how much has she cost you, the best, in three months?"

"I'm no longer with you?"

"I said: How much has it cost you in three months, the most charming of your mistresses – in cash, jewellery, suppers, dinners, theatres etc. In fact the full treatment?"

"How do I know?"

"You ought to know. Let's see, a reasonable average price. Five thousand francs a month; is that near enough right?"

"Yes ….. near enough."

"Well, my dear, give me now five thousand francs and I am yours for a month counting from this evening."

"You are mad."

"You can take it like that. Good night."

The countess left and went into her bedroom. The bed was turned down. A vague perfume lingered, impregnating the curtains.

The count appeared at the door:

"It smells very good here."

"Really? But nothing has been changed. I always use Spanish."

"Fancy that, it is amazing ….. it is very good."

"Maybe ….. but please leave because I am going to bed."

"Marguerite!"

"Get out!"

He came right in and sat down in an armchair.

The countess:

"Ah! It's like that then. Well, so much the worse for you."

Slowly she took off her evening blouse, freeing her bare white arms which she raised above her head to let her hair down in front of the mirror; under a mass of lace something pink appeared at the edge of her black silk corset.

The count got up quickly and came towards her.

The countess:

"Don't come near me or I will get angry!....."

He seized her with both arms and sought her lips.

Then she grabbed a glass of scented mouthwash from her dressing table and looking over her shoulder she threw it straight into her husband's face…

He recovered himself, spluttering furiously, murmuring:

"It's stupid."

"That may be ….. but you have my terms: five thousand francs."

"But that would be idiotic!....."

"Why?"

"How, why? A husband paying to sleep with his wife!....."

"Oh! ….. what cheap words you are using!....."

"Possibly. I repeat that it would be idiotic to pay one's wife, one's lawful wife."

"It is much more stupid to go paying trollops when one has a lawful wife."

"Maybe but I do not wish to be made ridiculous."

The countess sat down on her chaise longue. Slowly she pulled off her stockings, peeling them back like a snake's skin. Her pink leg emerged from the sheath of purple silk and she put her tiny foot on the carpet.

The count came a little closer and said in a tender voice:

""What a funny idea you had then?"

"What idea?"

"To ask me for five thousand francs."

"Nothing more natural. We are strangers to one another, are we not? But you want me. You cannot marry me because we are already married. So you will buy me for a little less perhaps than someone else. So think about it. This money, instead of going to a bit of skirt who will use it for I know not what, will stay in your home, in your household. And next, for an intelligent man, is there anything more enjoyable, more original than to pay his own wife. With illegitimate love, one only loves best what is expensive, very expensive. You will be giving to our love ..... legitimate love a new value, a flavour of debauchery, a ragout of naughtiness ..... pricing it ... like love on the market. Isn't it true?"

She got up almost naked and headed for her dressing room.

"Now, sir, clear off; or I will ring for my maid."

The count, standing up, perplexed and unhappy, looked at her and abruptly, threw his wallet at her head:

"There take it you beggar, there's six thousand there ..... but you know something?"

The countess picked up the money, counted it and in a quiet voice:

"What?"

"Don't get used to the idea."

She burst out laughing, and going towards him:

"Each month, sir, five thousand, or I will send you back to your trollops. And even if ..... if you are satisfied ..... I will ask you for an increase."

GOODBYE

The two friends were finishing their dinner. From the window of the café they could see the packed boulevard. They could feel the warm breath of wind which blew through Paris during these mild summer nights; they looked up at the passers-by and they had the urge to leave, to get away no matter where, under the trees and on moonlit river banks, to dream of glowworms and nightingales. One of them, Henri Simon, announced with a deep sigh:

"Ah! I am growing old. It is sad. In the past during nights like these, I would have felt devilishly passionate. To-day I only feel regrets. How life passes quickly."

He was already a little stout, aged forty-five perhaps and very bald.

The other one, Pierre Carnier, a touch older but thinner and more alive, took up the conversation:

As for me, old boy, I grew old without realising it in the least. I was always cheerful, vigorous, energetic and the rest. But as one looks at oneself in the mirror, we do not appreciate the workings of age because they are slow and regular and alter our appearance so gently that the changes are not felt. It is uniquely for this reason that we do not die of grief after only two or three years of deterioration – because we cannot appreciate it. To take it into account, it would be necessary to pass six months without looking at one's face – oh! Then what a blow!

And the women, my dear chap, how I pity them, the poor things! All their happiness, all their power, all their life lies in their beauty which lasts ten years.

So, as for me, I grew old without suspecting it. I thought I was practically an adolescent when I was nearly fifty. Having never experienced an illness of any sort, I went through life happily and serenely.

The revelation of my decline came to me in a simple and terrible fashion which laid me low for nearly six months ..... then I came to terms with it.

Like all men I had often been in love but really in love only once.

I had met her at the seaside at Etretat about twelve years ago, a little after the war.[1] Nothing is nicer than that beach in the morning, at bathing time. It was small, rounded like a horseshoe, backed by tall white cliffs, pierced with peculiar holes, that are known as the 'Portes', one of them huge, extending its giant's leg into the sea, the other rounded and crouching: the crowd of women assemble and gather there on that narrow tongue of shingle covering it with a dazzling array of bright dresses in that backdrop of high rocks. The sun beats right down on the cliff sides, on the parasols of every hue, on the greenish blue sea; and all that is gay, charming, smiling. One goes to sit down right next to the water and one watches the bathers. They come down dressed in a flannel bath robe, which they throw off with a pretty movement as they reach the fringe of surf produced by the small waves; then they go into the water with short quick steps, sometimes arrested by a delicious cold shiver when they stop to catch their breath.

Few really resist this bathing experience. It is there when one judges them from the calf to the bosom. Their exit especially shows up the weak ones even though seawater can be a potent assistance to flabby flesh.

The first time I saw the young woman like that I was captivated and seduced. She held good and firm, that one. Then there are some faces whose charm strikes us abruptly invades us. It seems that we have found the woman we have been born to love. I had that sensation and that shock.

I introduced myself and soon I was hooked like I have never been. She ravaged my heart. It is a frightening and delicious thing to submit to the domination of a woman. It is almost a torture and at the same time an unbelievable joy. Her look, her smile, the hair on the back of the neck wafted by the breeze, all the smallest lines on her face, the tiniest movement of her features delighted me, bowled me over, sent me crazy. She possessed me with her whole person, with her gestures, with her behaviour, even with the things she wore which became bewitching; I felt moved when I saw her veil on a table, her gloves thrown on to an armchair. Her dresses were inimitable. No-one had hats like hers.

She was married but the husband only came every Sunday to leave again on the Monday. Besides he left me indifferent. I was not jealous, I do not know why; never did a human being seem to have so little importance in my life, to attract less of my attention than that man.

How I loved her! She was so beautiful, young and elegant! It was the youth, the manners and even the freshness. I had never felt before like this – how a woman is pretty, distinguished, slim and delicate, being made for charm and grace. I had never understood what seductive beauty there is in the curve of a cheek, in the movement of a lip, in the shape of that silly organ we call the nose.

The affair lasted for three months, then I left for America, my heart crushed by despair. But the thought of her stayed with me, persistently, triumphantly. She possessed me from afar as she had done close to home. The years passed. I did not forget her. Her captivating image remained before my eyes and in my heart. My affection remained faithful to her, now a quiet affection, now something like an adored memory of the most beautiful and attractive object in my life.

Twelve years are so little in a man's existence! One doesn't realise that they are gone! They come one after the other, the years, swiftly and gently, slowly and hurriedly, each one is long and over so soon! They add up so quickly, they leave so little trace behind them, they vanish so completely that one looks round to view the time passed, we see nothing, and we do not understand how it is that we have become old.

It really seemed to me that just a few months were separating me from the delightful season on the beach at Etretat.

Last spring I went to dinner with friends at Maisons-Lafitte.

As the train was leaving, a big lady climbed into my carriage, escorted by four small girls. I scarcely glanced at this very large and round mother hen with a moon face framed by a hat with ribbons.

She was perspiring freely, breathless from having walked fast. The children started to chatter. I opened my paper and began to read.

We had just past Asnières, when my neighbour suddenly said to me:

"Excuse me, sir, are you not Monsieur Carnier?"

"Yes, Madame."

Then she started to laugh, a happy laugh of a nice woman, and yet a little sad.

"Don't you recognise me?"

I hesitated. In fact In fact I had an impression that I had seen that face somewhere; but where? And when? I replied:

"Yes ….. and no ….. I certainly know you but I do not recall your name."

She blushed a little:

"Madame Julie Lefèvre."

Never have I received a shock like that. In a second it seemed that for me everything was at an end! My only feeling was that a veil had been torn apart in front of my eyes and that I was going to discover some frightful and distressing things.

It was her! This common woman, her? And she had hatched these four girls since I saw her last. And these small beings astonished me as much as their mother herself. They came out of her. They were already grown up and had taken their place in life, while, she, that marvellously slender and pretty woman no longer counted. It seemed that I had seen her only yesterday and now I found her again like this! Was it possible? A violent pain seized my heart, as well as a revulsion against nature itself, an irrational indignation against this brutal work, this despicable destruction.

In a panic, I looked at her. Then I took her hand; tears came into my eyes. I mourned her youth. I mourned her death. For I did not know this big lady, not at all.

Also moved she stammered:

"I have really changed, haven't I? What can one do, everything carries on. You can see that I have become a mother. Goodbye to the rest, it is finished. Oh! I really thought that you would not recognise me if we were ever to meet again. Besides you have changed as well. I needed a little time to make sure I was not mistaken. You have become quite pale. Think about it; here we are twelve years on. Oh! Twelve years! My eldest daughter is already ten."

I looked at the child. I discovered in her some of her mother's old charm, but also something uncertain, half formed, something to follow. And life appeared to me rapid like a train which passes.

We arrived at Maisons-Lafitte. I kissed my old friend's hand. I could find nothing to say to her except terrible banalities. I was too upset to speak.

In the evening, all alone at home I looked at myself in the mirror for a long time, a very long time. I ended by remembering what I had been, by imagining my brown moustache, my dark hair and the youthful appearance of my face. Now I was old. Goodbye.

THE LANDLADY

I was living at the time, said Georges Kervelen, in a furnished house, Rue Saints-Pères.

When my parents decided that I would study law in Paris, long discussions took place to settle everything. To start with the total of my allowance had been fixed at two thousand five hundred francs but my poor mother took fright and explained to my father: "If he spends all this money foolishly and will not take enough food, his health will suffer badly. Young people these days are capable of anything."

So it was decided to look for some lodgings, a modest but comfortable boarding-house and my family would pay the fees each month directly.

I had never left Quimper before. I wanted everything that one usually wants at my age and I intended to enjoy myself in every way.

Some neighbours who were asked their advice referred to a fellow countrywoman, Madame Kergaran, who took in lodgers. My father dealt with this respectable person by letter and I arrived at her house one evening with my suitcase.

Madame Kergaran was around forty. She was forceful, very forceful. She spoke with the voice of a drill-sergeant and decided every question in a word – simple and definite. Her house was quite narrow with only a single exit to the street. Looking at each floor, it was like a ladder of windows or rather like a slice of a house sandwiched between two others.

The landlady lived on the first floor with her maid; they took their meals on the second; four Breton lodgers had the third and fourth. I had the two rooms on the fifth.

A little dark spiral staircase led to these two attic rooms. Every day without fail Madame Kergaran climbed up and down these spiral stairs. She busied herself with these lodgings in this chest of drawers like a captain on board his ship. She went into each room, one after another ten times, inspecting everything, with an amazing blaze of words, making sure that the beds had been well made, the coats well brushed and that the service left nothing to be desired. In fact she looked after her lodgers like a mother, better than a mother.

Soon I got to know my four fellow countrymen; two were studying medicine and the two others law, but they all put up with the despotic rule of the landlady. They were frightened of her like a petty thief was frightened of a country policeman.

As far as I was concerned, straightaway I felt the need for independence, for I am a rebel by nature. First, I declared that I wished to come in at times which suited me, for Madame Kergaran had fixed midnight as the limit. At this request, she turned on me her steely eye and stated:

"It is not possible. I cannot tolerate Annette being wakened all night. You have nothing to do out of the house past a certain time."

I replied with firmness: "According to the law, Madame, you are obliged to stay open for me all the hours. If you refuse, I will put it on record with the local police and I will go and sleep at a hotel at your expense as is my right. You are therefore compelled to keep open for me or expel me. The door or goodbye. Choose."

In posing these conditions, I was laughing up my sleeve at her. After preliminary amazement, she wanted to negotiate but I was intractable and she gave way. We agreed that I should have a pass key, but on the formal condition that no-one else would know about it.

My forcefulness made a salutary impression on her and from then on she treated me with marked favour. She paid me little courtesies, attentions and kindnesses and even with brusque affection which did not displease me. Sometimes when I was having some fun, I gave her a surprise hug, anything for the smart slap she immediately gave me. When I happened to give her a quick kiss on the cheek, her raised hand passed over the top of my head with the speed of a bullet, and in dodging out of the way, I was laughing like a madman, while she was shouting: "Ah! The rascal! I will get even with you for that."

We were becoming a couple of friends.

But the thing was that I got to know a young girl in the street, a shop assistant.

You are familiar with these passing infatuations in Paris. One day on the way to the school, you meet a young person with her hair down walking arm in arm with a girlfriend before returning to work. You exchange a look and you experience that little tremor which the glance of certain girls give you. It is one of those delightful things in life, that swift physical sympathy which an encounter produces; suddenly you submit to that light and delicate seduction, that contact with a person born to please you and be loved by you. She will be loved a little or a lot, what does it matter? It is in her nature to respond to your secret need for love. From the first time that you se that face, that mouth, that hair, that smile, with a sweet and delicious joy you feel their spell getting to you; you experience a kind of happy well-being overtaking you and that sudden awakening of a still confused affection which pushes you towards that unknown female. It seems that there might be in her a call to which you are replying, an attraction which appeals to you; it seems that you have known her for a long time, that you have seen her before and that you know what she is thinking.

The next day at the same time you go down the same street again. You see her again. Then you come back the following day and again the day after that. At last you get talking and the infatuation follows its regular course like an illness.

So at the end of three weeks, with Emma I was at the stage which precedes the fall. In fact it would have come sooner if I had known of some place to bring it about. My girlfriend lived with her family and absolutely refused to cross the threshold of a furnished hotel. I racked my brains to find a means, a device, an opportunity. In the end I opted for a desperate solution and I decided to get her to come to my room one evening as an excuse for a cup of tea. Madame Kergaran went to bed every day at ten o'clock. So with the aid of my pass key I would be able to come in without making a noise and without attracting attention. We would come back down again in the same way at the end of an hour or two.

Emma accepted my invitation after a little persuasion.

I spent a bad day. I was not easy in my mind. I feared complications, some awful scandal…. The evening came. I went out and dropped into a brasserie where I had two cups of coffee and four or five quick drinks to give me courage. Then I went for a stroll on the boulevard Saint-Michel. I heard the clock strike ten and then half past. Slowly I headed for the place of our rendez-vous. She was already waiting for me. She took my arm in an affectionate way and we went off quite gently towards my residence. As I approached the door, my anxiety was growing. I was thinking: "Provided that Madame Kergaran has gone to bed."

I said to Emma two or three times: "Above all, don't make a sound on the stairs."

She started to laugh: "So, you are really scared of being heard."

"No, but I don't want to wake up my neighbour who is seriously ill."

So here we were at Saints-Peres street. I was approaching my lodgings with that kind of apprehension that one has on visiting the dentist. All the windows were dark. Doubtless everyone was asleep. I breathed again. I opened the door with the caution of a burglar. I ushered my companion through and relocked the door. I went up the stairs on tiptoe, lighting some matches so that the girl would not make a false step.

In passing the landlady's room I felt my heart beating fast. At last we were on the second floor, then the third, then the fifth. I entered my rooms. Victory!

Yet I only dared to speak in a whisper and I took off my boots so as not to make any noise. The tea was prepared on a spirit lamp and we drank it from the corner of my chest of drawers. Then I became insistent ....pressing .... And little by little, as in a game, one by one I removed my girlfriend's clothes. Resisting, blushing, she yielded, always delaying the fatal and delightful moment.

I swear that she had no more on than a short white slip, when all of a sudden my door opened and Madame Kergaran appeared, a candle in her hand wearing exactly the same thing as Emma.

I jumped back from her, panic stricken and still standing I looked at the two women who were staring at each other. What was going to happen?

In a haughty tone that I did not recognise, the landlady pronounced: "I do not want girls in my house, Monsieur Kervelen."

I stammered: "But, Madame Kergaran, Mademoiselle is only my friend. She was just having a cup of tea."

The large woman replied: "One does not put oneself in a nightdress to take a cup of tea. You are going to get this person to leave immediately."

Emma, dismayed, started to cry and hid her face in her skirt. As for me I lost my head, not knowing what to do or what to say. The landlady with irresistible authority, added: "Help Mademoiselle to be dressed and see her out immediately."

To be sure I had nothing else to do, so I picked up the dress which had fallen on the floor round the girl like a burst balloon and passed it over her head. With infinite trouble I tried hard to fasten and adjust it. She helped me, flustered and crying all the time; she was in too much of a rush and made all kinds of mistakes, no longer knowing where to find the laces and the button holes. Madame Kergaran upright and impassive the candle in her hand in the severe posture of a judge lit up our efforts.

Now Emma was really rushing her movements, running about wildly, knotting, pinning, lacing and re-attaching furiously, harassed by the imperative need to flee and without even buttoning her boots, she ran past the landlady and hurled herself down the stairs. I was following in slippers, half undressed myself, repeating: "Emma, listen, Mademoiselle, listen."

I really felt that I needed to say something, but I couldn't find the words.

I caught her just at the street door; I wanted to take her in my arms but she pushed me away violently, stammering in a low and nervous voice: "Leave me …. leave me …. Don't touch me."

Then she rushed off into the street slamming the door behind her.

I turned round. Madame Kergaran was standing at the level of the first floor and I re-climbed the stairs slowly, expecting everything and ready for everything.

The landlady's room was open; she made me come in, declaring in a severe tone: "I have to speak to you, Monsieur Kervelen."

I stood before her with my head lowered. She put the candle on the mantelpiece; then with her arms folded across her ample bosom which was scarcely covered by her white nightdress, she said:

"Ah, so that's it, Monsieur Kervelen, so you take my house for a brothel!"

I was not proud; I murmured: "But no, Madame Kergaran, you must not be angry. You see, you know very well what a young man gets up to."

She replied: "I know that I do not want creatures like that in my house, do you hear. I know that I will have my roof and the reputation of my house respected, do you hear? I know …."

She went on speaking for at least twenty minutes, piling up reasons for her indignation, overwhelming me with the good name of her house and piercing me with biting reproaches.

Me, (man is a peculiar animal) instead of listening to her, I was looking at her. I was no longer hearing a word, not one word. She had a superb bust, that woman, firm, white and solid, a little large perhaps, but tending to produce tinglings in the back. Truthfully, I should never have doubted that she had the same attributes under her landlady's woollen dress but now, undressed she seemed ten years younger. And you see I was feeling quite peculiar, quite …. How shall I put it? ….quite stirred up. Suddenly, in front of her, I was recalling my situation ….. interrupted a quarter of an hour earlier in my room.

Now, over there in her room behind her in the alcove, I was looking at her bed. It was unmade and crumpled and the hollow in the sheets was showing the weight of the body that had lain there. I was thinking how nice and very warm it must have been, warmer than another bed. Why warmer? I have no idea. It must have been something to do with the opulence of the body which had rested there.

What is more troubling and delightful than an unmade bed? That was by far the most exhilarating thing and it was making my skin tingle.

She was still going on, but now more quietly and she was speaking more as a close and kind friend who was asking for no more than an apology.

I stammered: "Look …. look ….Madame Kergaran …. look .." And as she fell silent, waiting my reply, I grabbed her with both my arms and started to embrace her and the kisses were like those of a man who was starving and had been expecting them for a long time.

She struggled and turned her head away, without being terribly angry, repeating mechanically as was her custom: "Oh! You rascal ….you rascal you ras …"

She was unable to complete the word. With an effort, I had lifted her up and carried her, squeezed tightly against me – one can be brutally vigorous at certain moments, you know!

Without letting her go I came up against the edge of the bed and fell on top of it.

In fact it was very nice and very warm in her bed.

An hour later the candle had gone out and the landlady got up to light another one and as she came back and snuggled up beside me, sliding her big and clubby leg under the sheets, she declared in a cuddly, satisfied and perhaps grateful voice: "Oh! You rascal … you rascal ………!

A MEMORY

How they come back to me –those memories of youth under the sweet touch of early sunshine! It is a time of life when everything is cheerful, good, delightful, intoxicating. How exquisite they are those memories of past springtime!

You, my friends, my old pals, do you recall those joyful years when life was a laugh and a triumph? Do you remember the days of wandering round Paris gloriously broke, the walks in the green woods, our exhilaration in the fabulous atmosphere of the cafés on the banks of the Seine, our experiences of love so commonplace and so delicious?

I want to mention one of those adventures. It was twelve years ago; already it seems like a long time ago, very long ago now that I am seeing it from another period in my life before the turning point, that ugly turning point from where I have suddenly caught sight of the end.

Then I was twenty-five. I had just arrived in Paris. I had a job in a government office and to me Sundays seemed like extra special holidays, full of exuberant happiness although nothing surprising ever occurred.

To-day every day is a Sunday. But I regret the time when I only had one Sunday each week. How good it was! I used to have six francs to spend!

*

I woke early on that particular Sunday morning with that feeling of freedom which every employee knows so well, that feeling of release, rest, peace and independence.

I opened the window. It was a marvellous day. Over the city there was a cloudless blue sky full of sunlight and swallows.

I got dressed very quickly and departed, intending to spend the day in the woods and to breathe in the foliage; for by birth I was a country person, having been brought up in the fields and under the trees.

Paris was stirring, full of joy in the warmth and the light. The facades of the houses were shining; the canaries of the door-keepers were singing in their cages at the tops of their voices; there was gaiety around the street, brightening up faces and producing a laugh everywhere; it was as if there was in every person and every object a mysterious satisfaction under the bright rising sun.

I reached the Seine to catch the 'Hirondelle' which would drop me at Saint-Cloud.

How I loved that wait on the jetty expecting the boat! I imagined that I was going to depart for the end of the world, for new and wonderful lands. I saw it appearing; it was that boat over there under the arch of the second bridge, quite small with a plume of smoke, then getting bigger and bigger, continually growing larger and in my mind it took on the aspect of an ocean liner.

It came alongside and I boarded.

People in their Sunday best were already on top, in dazzling outfits, with ribbons flying and big ruddy faces. I placed myself right up forward, standing up, watching the quays, the trees, the bridges and the houses flying past. Suddenly I saw the huge viaduct of the Pont-du-Jour which barred the river. It was the end of Paris and the beginning of the countryside and the Seine behind the double row of arches immediately grew wider as if it had been granted space and freedom; all of sudden it was transformed into a beautiful, peaceful river, flowing across plains, through the middle of fields, past the foot of wooded hills, along the edge of forests.

Having passed between two islands, the 'Hirondelle' followed a winding hillside, whose green slopes were dotted with white houses. A voice announced: "Bas-Meudon," then further on: "Sèvres," and again still further: "Saint-Cloud."

I disembarked and, after a brisk walk through the small town, I followed the road which led to the woods. I had brought a map of the outskirts of Paris with me so that I would not get lost in the tracks which criss-crossed in every direction the small forests where Parisians took their walks.

As soon as I was in the shade, I studied my route which, needless to say, seemed to me perfectly straight forward. I would turn right, then left and then left again and I would arrive at Versailles in the evening for dinner.

Then I started to walk slowly under the new foliage, drinking in the savoury air scented with the buds and the sap. I took small strides oblivious of the paperwork, the office, the boss, the colleagues, the files, dreaming of happy things which could not miss happening to me and of every hidden unknown event which the future might bring. I was struck by a thousand childhood memories which these country paths re-awakened in me. I was going along totally immersed in the sweet smelling spell, under the lively spell, the throbbing spell of woods warmed by the high June sun.

Occasionally I sat down to look at all kinds of small flowers along the embankment – whose names I used to know a long time ago. I recognised them all; they might have been just the same as those I had seen in the countryside in the past. They were yellow, red, violet and cute, mounted on long stalks or glued to the ground. There were insects of all colours and shapes, squat, elongated, of extraordinary construction, dreadful and microscopic monsters; peacefully they climbed up the blades of grass which gave way under their weight.

Next I slept for a few hours in a ditch and set off again rested and fortified by the nap.

In front of me a delightful alley opened up above which the slightly thinner foliage allowed drops of sunlight to rain down on the ground lighting up the white daisies. It stretched out endlessly calm and empty. Alone, a huge, solitary, buzzing hornet was following it, stopping from time to time to drink in a flower which bent down underneath it, then setting off again almost immediately to resettle still further away. Its enormous body looked like brown velvet with yellow stripes, supported by transparent wings inordinately small.

Then all of a sudden I saw at the end of the alley two people, a man and a woman coming towards me. Annoyed at the prospect of being disturbed on my peaceful walk, I was going to sink down out of sight in the undergrowth when it seemed that they were calling me. In fact the woman was waving her umbrella and the man in shirt-sleeves with his coat over one arm was raising his other one as a signal of distress.

I went towards them. They were both very red, walking hurriedly, she with short, quick steps, he with long strides. You could see on their faces fatigue and bad temper.

The woman immediately asked me:

"Sir, can you tell me were we are? My imbecile of a husband, pretending to know this area perfectly has got us lost."

Confidently I replied:

"Madame, you are going towards Saint-Cloud and you are showing your back to Versailles."

With a look of irritated pity for her spouse, she replied:

"What! Versailles is behind us? But it is precisely there where we wish to have dinner."

"Me too, Madame, I am going there."

Shrugging her shoulders, she pronounced several times:

"My God! My God! My God!" with that tone of haughty scorn which women use to express their exasperation.

She was quite a young and pretty brunette with a hint of a moustache on her lip.

As for him, he was sweating and wiping his forehead. They were certainly a petit-bourgeois Parisian couple. The man looked exhausted, crestfallen and depressed.

He murmured:

"But, my dear ….. it was you ….."

She did not let him finish:

"It was me! ….. Ah! It is me now. Was it me who wanted to set off without information pretending that I would always find my way? Was it me who wanted to turn right at the top of the hill, swearing that I recognised the track? Was it me who was in charge of Cachou?"

She had not finished speaking when her husband as if he might have been struck by madness, let out a piercing cry, a long wild cry which could not be written down in any language but which sounded like "tiitiiit."

The young woman who seemed neither astonished nor moved, carried on:

"No, really, there are some people who are too stupid; they make out that they always know everything. Was it me last year who took the Dieppe train instead of the one to Le Havre, tell me, was it me? Was it me who bet that M. Letournier lived in Martyrs street? ….. Was it me who refused to believe that Céleste was a thief?"

And she continued in a fury, talking at a surprising speed, piling up all sorts of accusations, the most unexpected and the most damning, producing evidence from every intimate situation of their life together; she criticised her husband for all his actions, all his ideas, all his behaviour, all his attempts, all his efforts and his life from the time they were married right up to the present moment.

He tried to stop her and calm her down. He stammered:

"But, my dear ….. it is pointless ….. we are making an exhibition of ourselves in front of the gentleman….. None of that is of any interest to the gentleman."

Then he turned with a pathetic look towards the undergrowth as if he wished to probe its mysterious and peaceful depths so he could throw himself inside it, flee and hide himself from view; also from time to time he uttered a new cry, a "tiitiiit," prolonged and very shrill. I reckoned this habit to be the result of some nervous disease.

All of a sudden, the young woman turned towards me, and changing her tone with remarkable rapidity, said:

"If the gentleman will kindly permit it, we will go along the route with him so that we do not go astray again and risk having to sleep in the woods."

I bowed; she took my arm and started to talk of a thousand things, of herself, her life, her family and her business. They sold gloves in Saint-Lazare street.

Her husband walked beside her, continually shooting frenzied glances into the dense forest and crying "tiitiiit" every other second.

In the end I asked him:

"Why do you cry like that?"

With a dismayed and desperate expression, he replied:

"It is my poor dog which I have lost."

"What? You have lost your dog?"

"Yes. He was hardly a year old and had never left the shop. I wanted to take him for a walk in the woods. He had never seen grass and leaves and he went crazy. He started running and barking and he disappeared into the forest. I should also say that he has been very scared of the railway and that could have made him lose his senses. Even if I call him, he doesn't come back. He is going to die of starvation in there."

Without turning towards her husband, the young woman stated:

"If you hadn't let him off his lead that would never have happened. When one is stupid like you, one doesn't have a dog."

Timidly he murmured:

"But, my dear, it was you ….."

She stopped him dead and looking into his eyes as if she was going to tear them out, she began again to hurl countless reproaches into his face.

Evening fell. The light mist which covers the countryside at dusk slowly spread; there was something romantic in the air, produced by that feeling of particular coolness which fills the woods when night approaches.

Suddenly the young man stopped and frantically tapping his sides, said:

"Oh! I think I've……"

She looked at him:

"Well, what now!"

"I was not paying attention that I had my coat over my arm."

"Well?"

"I have lost my wallet….. My money was inside."

She shook with anger and choked with indignation.

"There was more than that missing. How stupid you are! Really stupid! Is it possible to have married such an idiot! Well, go and look for it and make sure you find it again. As for me, I am going to get to Versailles with the gentleman. I have no intention of sleeping in the woods."

Gently he replied:

"Yes, my dear; where will I find you?"

I had been recommended a restaurant. I told him where it was.

The husband turned round and went off; he was bending over and his anxious eyes were running over the ground; at every moment he shouted "tiitiiit!"

He took a long time to disappear; in the far distance down the alley the lengthening shadows blotted him out. Soon his silhouette could no longer be distinguished but for a long time we heard his pathetic "tiit tiiit! Tiit tiiit!" And as the night grew darker the more high pitched it became.

As for me I went off at a lively pace, a happy pace in the mildness of dusk with this little unknown woman on my arm.

I was searching for some gallant words without finding any. I was dumb, disturbed, delighted.

But suddenly a main road cut across our alley. To the right in a little valley I saw quite a town.

So where on earth were we?

A man was passing. I questioned him. He replied:

"Bougival."

I was dumbfounded:

"What! Bougival? Are you sure?"

"What the hell, I'm from there!"

The little woman laughed madly.

I suggested getting a carriage to take us to Versailles. She replied:

"Good God, no! It is too funny, and I am too hungry. Actually I am quite calm. As for my husband, he will always cope. It is quite a bonus to be relieved of him for a few hours."

So we entered a restaurant at the edge of the water and I dared to take a private room.

My God, she got really very tight, sang, drank champagne and committed all kind of indiscretions ..... and even the biggest of them all.

It was my first adultery.

FATHER BONIFACE'S CRIME

It was a day when Boniface the postman reckoned as he left the post office, that his round would be shorter than usual and he was feeling in a good mood. He was responsible for the houses in the countryside surrounding the market town of Vireville and when he used to return in the evenings from his long tiring trek, sometimes his legs had done more than forty kilometres.

So the delivery would be done quickly; he could even stroll a little along the way and be back about three hours after checking in. What luck!

He left the town on the Sennemare road and started his round. It was in June, when the land was green and everything blooming, the right month to be in the vast fields of crops.

Dressed in his blue smock and with his black kepi with the red stripes on his head he crossed the fields of colza, barley or corn, down narrow tracks; submerged up to his shoulders in the crops, his head, sticking out, appeared to be floating on a calm and verdant sea on which a light breeze was making gentle waves.

He entered the farms by way of the wooden fence situated on the embankments which were in the shade of two rows of beech trees; he used to greet the farmer by name: "Good morning, master Chicot," as he handed over his paper – 'Le Petit Normand'. The farmer used to wipe his hand on the seat of his trousers as he received the broadsheet, and then slipped it into his pocket to read at his leisure after the midday meal. The dog, lodged in a barrel at the foot of a gnarled apple tree, barked furiously pulling on its chain; the postman without waiting , departed at a military pace on his long legs, his left arm over his satchel and his right

manipulating his stick which proceeded like him in an uninter-
rupted and harmonious fashion.

He distributed his letters and papers in the hamlet of Sennemare; then he went on across the fields to deliver the post to
the tax inspector who lived in a little isolated house a kilometre
from the town.

It was a new tax inspector, M. Chapatis who had arrived only
a week ago and had only recently been married.

He used to receive a Paris newspaper and sometimes Boniface, the postman, used to glance at the headlines before deliver-
ing it to its destination.

So on this day he opened his bag, took out the paper, slipped
it out of its wrapper and, while still walking along, started to
read it.… The first page hardly interested him; politics left him
cold; he always skipped the financial page but he was very keen
on various news reports.

On this day he was very well satisfied. He was even so deeply
stirred by the story of a crime committed in the house of a game-
keeper that he stopped in the middle of a field of clover to read it
slowly. The details were awful. A lumberjack while passing the
house in the forest in the morning had noticed a little blood on
the doorstep as if somebody had had a nosebleed. The warden
must have shot a rabbit last night, he thought; but on getting
closer, he spotted that the door was still open and that the lock
had been broken.

Then overcome with fright, he ran to the village to warn the
mayor who summoned up the local policeman and school teach-
er as reinforcements; the four men had returned together. They
had found the forester in front of the mantelpiece with his throat
cut, his wife under the bed strangled and their little six year old
girl suffocated between two mattresses.

Boniface was so upset by the thought of these murders whose
horrible circumstances were being revealed to him blow by blow
that he felt weak in the knees. He exclaimed loudly:

"Good God, honestly there must be people about who are
villains!"

Then he replaced the paper in the wrapper and set off again, his head full of the vision of the crime. He soon reached M. Chapatis's residence; he opened the small garden gate and approached the house. It was a low building with only a ground floor and surmounted by a roof with an attic. It was set apart from the nearest neighbouring house by at least five hundred metres.

Then the postman went up the two steps of the door, put his hand on the latch and tried to open it; but he reckoned it was locked shut. Next he spotted that the shutters had not been pulled back and that no one had yet gone out that day.

He was worried because M. Chapatis since his arrival was usually awake quite early. Boniface pulled out his watch. It was still only ten minutes past seven, so he was nearly an hour earlier than normal. No matter, the tax inspector should have been up and about.

Then he made a tour round the house, walking carefully as if he might be running into some sort of danger. He noticed nothing suspicious, only a man's footprint in the strawberry bed.

But suddenly he stopped still while passing a window, paralysed with anxiety. Someone was groaning inside the house. He got closer, and stepping astride a border of thyme, he stuck his ear against the ventilator to listen better. Certainly someone was groaning. He could very well hear long sighs of pain, a sort of death rattle, a noise of a struggle. Then the groans became louder, more repetitive and, still more accentuated, they changed into screams.

Then Boniface was no longer in doubt that a crime was being committed in the tax inspector's home; he left as fast as his legs could carry him, recrossed the small garden rushed across the fields, across the crops, running, panting and shaking his post bag which was bouncing up and down on his back; finally, exhausted, breathless and frantic he arrived at the door of the police station.

The brigadier Malatour was repairing a broken chair with some nails and a hammer. The constable Rautier was holding it between his legs and offering up a nail at the edge of the break; then the brigadier, his eyes wide open and watering with concentration, was hitting the fingers of his subordinate with every blow.

As soon as he saw them, the postman cried out:

"Come quick, they are murdering the tax inspector, quick, quick!"

The two men stopped their work and raised their hands in the manner of people who are surprised at being disturbed.

Boniface, seeing that, although surprised they were hardly in a hurry, repeated:

"Quick, quick! The thieves are in the house. I heard screams. There is no time."

The brigadier, putting his hammer down, asked:

"What is it that has given you cognizance of these facts?"

The postman replied:

"I was going to deliver the newspaper with two letters when I noticed that the door was closed and the tax inspector was not yet up. I made a tour of the house to investigate, and I heard groans as if someone was being strangled or was having their throat cut; then I departed at all speed to look for you. There is no time."

The brigadier, standing up, went on:

"And you did not personally go to the rescue?"

The astounded postman replied:

"I feared that I was not in numbers sufficient."

Then the policeman was convinced and announced:

"Give me time to get changed and I will follow you."

He went inside the station followed by the constable who carried the chair.

They reappeared almost immediately, and all three set off at a military pace to the scene of the crime.

On approaching the house, as a precaution they slowed their step and the brigadier drew his revolver; then very quietly they entered the garden and went up to the side of the house; there was no sign to indicate that the criminals had left. The door remained shut, the windows closed.

"We will take them," the brigadier whispered.

Father Boniface, quivering with emotion, led him round to the other side and pointed out the ventilator:

"It is there," he said.

The brigadier advanced alone and struck his ear against the piece of wood. The other two waited, their eyes fixed on him, ready for everything. He stayed there a long time motionless, listening. To get his head closer to the wooden flap, he had to take off his three cornered hat and he was holding it in his right hand.

What was he hearing? His impassive face revealed nothing, but suddenly his moustache twitched, his cheeks creased as if in a silent laugh and, stepping back again over the border of thyme, he returned to the two men who were looking at him in amazement.

Then walking on tiptoe he made a sign to them to follow him; and coming back to the front porch, he motioned to Boniface to slip the paper and letters under the door.

The dumbfounded postman obediently complied.

"And now let's be on our way," said the brigadier.

But as soon as they were on the other side of the fence with a sarcastic and mocking smile, his eyes twitching and shining with joy, he said:

"What an idiot you are, you!"

The old man asked:

"What? I heard, I swear to you I heard."

The policeman, going no further, burst out laughing. He was laughing as to if to choke himself. His two hands were clasped together across his stomach; his eyes were full of tears and with frightful contortions round his nose. The two others watched him, panic stricken.

Since he could not stop laughing, nor speak, nor make them understand what it was, he made a gesture, a popular and impudent gesture.

As they still did not understand, he repeated it several times in succession, pointing with a signal from his head at the house which was still closed up.

And his constable, in his turn, suddenly understood and collapsed in huge mirth.

The old man stood stupidly between the two of them who were doubled up with laughter.

Finally the brigadier calmed down, and giving Boniface a smart punch in the stomach like someone will do when joking, cried:

"Ah! What a practical joker, the devil of a practical joke. I will report it as the crime of father Boniface!"

The postman opened his two enormous eyes and repeated:

"I swear to you that I heard."

The brigadier started to guffaw again, while his constable was sitting on the grass beside the ditch so he could laugh more freely.

"Ah! You heard. And your wife, is it like that when you murder her, what, you old joker?"

"My wife ….. yes, she yells if I give her a wallop ….. but yells, that is all. So was it M. Chapatis beating his wife?"

The brigadier delirious with amusement, turned him round by the shoulders like a rag doll and whispered something in his ear. The other one remained stupid with astonishment.

Then the old man was thoughtful and murmured:

"No ….. not like that … not at all like that ….. never like that … mine, she says nothing ….. I would never have believed it … if it is possible ….. I could have sworn that it was a woman being tortured."

And confused, bewildered and ashamed, he continued on his route across the fields while the constable and the brigadier carried on laughing, shouting out juicy barrack room jokes from afar and watched his black kepi getting further away across the calm sea of crops.

BOMBARD

Simon Bombard often found it rough, life! He was born with an incredible aptitude for doing nothing and with an exaggerated wish not to frustrate this vocation. Every mental or physical effort, every movement carried out on a task seemed to him to be beyond his abilities. As soon as he heard talk of a serious enterprise, he became vague and his mind was incapable of concentration or even of attention.

Son of a novelty merchant from Caen, they used to say in his family that it was easy for him up to the age of twenty five.

But since his parents were always nearer to bankruptcy than to fortune, he suffered horribly from a lack of money.

Tall, broad shouldered with red sideburns Norman fashion, he had a ruddy complexion with blue eyes; he was both silly and cheerful and already stout; he dressed with the elegance of a rowdy provincial on holiday. He laughed, shouted and gesticulated on every occasion, flaunting his tumultuous good humour with the assurance of a travelling salesman. He considered that life existed solely for joking and playing the fool, and as soon as it was necessary for him to put a brake on his brawling pleasure, he fell into a sort of stupid lethargy and was even incapable of feeling sad.

His need for cash plagued him and he was in the habit of repeating a statement which became celebrated amongst his entourage:

"For ten thousand francs of private income, I would do anything."

Then each year he used to go and spend fifteen days at Trouville. He called it 'doing his season.'

He installed himself with some cousins who lent him a room, and from the day he arrived to the day he departed, he used to take a walk along the boards which ran the length of the sandy beach.

He walked with a confident step, with his hands in his pockets or behind his back, always dressed in loose fitting jackets, light coloured waistcoats and loud ties, his hat over one ear and a cheap cigar in the corner of his mouth.

He went along brushing past elegant women, looking the men up and down and giving them a hearty slap on the back and he was searching ….. searching ….. for he was always searching.

He was looking for a woman and he was relying on his looks and his physique. He used to say to himself:

"What the devil, amongst the heaps of women who come here, I will end up finding my bargain." And he searched with the nose of a hunting dog, the flair of a Norman, sure that he would recognise her; he only had to spot her, the lady who would make him rich.

*

It was on Monday morning when he muttered:

"Well …. well …. Well."

It was superb weather, one of those golden and blue days in the month of July when you could say that it was pouring with heat. The huge beach was full of people; the dresses, the colours looked like a flower garden of women; the fishing boats with their tan sails, almost motionless under the high ten o'clock sun were reflected upside down in the blue water and almost seemed to be sleeping. They stayed there opposite the wooden jetty, some quite close, some further out and some even farther out; they did not stir as if overwhelmed by the idleness of a summer's day, too nonchalant to make for the open sea or even to return to port. Over there in the distance the cliffs of Le Havre could be seen in the haze with two white specks which were the lighthouses at Sainte-Adresse.

He was saying to himself:

"Well, well, well!" For the third time he had run into her, and he sensed that she was also looking at him; it was the mature, experienced and brazen look of a woman who was on offer.

He had already noticed her on preceding days, for also she seemed to be in search for somebody. It was an Englishwoman tall enough and a little thin, an arrogant Englishwoman, in whom travels and circumstances have produced a certain masculinity. However, not bad, walking primly with a short step, she was dressed simply and soberly but with an odd sort of hairstyle like they all have. She had fine eyes, and prominent cheekbones, which were a little red. Her teeth were too large and always showing.

When he arrived in the vicinity of the harbour, he retraced his steps to see if he would run into her one more time. He met her and threw her a passionate glance as if to say:

"Well, here I am."

But how was he to speak to her?

He returned a fifth time and saw her again. She came up to him face to face and dropped her umbrella.

He shot forward, picked it up and presented it to her:

"Allow me Madame."

She replied:

"Hi! You are awfully kind."

They looked at each other. They no longer knew what to say. She had blushed.

Then growing bolder, he announced:

"Look, what beautiful weather!"

She murmured:

"Rather! Delicious!"

Embarrassed, they remained facing each other; but neither of them were contemplating going away. It was she who had the boldness to ask:

"Are you round here for long?"

Smiling, he replied:

"Oh! Yes, as long as I want."

Then, quickly, he suggested:

"Will you come as far as the pier? It is so nice there these days."

She said simply:

"I would love to."

And they went off side by side, she upright with her prim step, he with his swaying gait like a strutting turkey cock.

*

Three months later the eminent tradesmen of Caen received one morning a large white invitation which said:

'Monsieur and Madame Prosper Bombard have the honour to invite you to the wedding of their son, Monsieur Simon Bombard and Madame Kate Robertson, widow.'

And on the other side:

'Madame Kate Robertson has the honour to invite you to her marriage with Monsieur Simon Bombard.'

*

They settled in Paris.

The fortune of the wife amounted to fifteen thousand francs of income net. Simon wanted four hundred francs a month for his personal needs. He had to demonstrate that his affectionate feelings merited this sacrifice; he proved it easily and obtained what he asked. Young Madame Bombard – certainly she was no longer young and her complexion had suffered; but she had a way of requiring things which made refusal impossible.

She used to say in her deliberately serious English accent:

"Hey! Simon, we are going to bed". This made Simon go to the bed, like a dog ordered to its basket. Throughout the day and the night she knew how to insist on everything in a manner which encouraged opposition.

She didn't get angry; she never shouted or made a scene. She never appeared irritated, wounded or even flustered. She knew how to communicate, that was all and, incidentally, she spoke in a tone that brooked no argument.

On more than one occasion Simon became almost reluctant; but in the face of the curt and imperious wishes of this unusual woman, he always ended up by giving way.

However he found the conjugal kisses monotonous and perfunctionary and as he had the wherewithal in his pocket to go for bigger excitements, he was soon indulging himself to the full but with a thousand precautions.

Madame Bombard was conscious of this without guessing exactly and one evening she announced that she had rented a house in Mantes where they would live in future.

Life became harder. He tried various distractions which did not succed in compensating for his heartfelt need for female conquests.

He tried fishing with the rod and line and he knew how to tell the difference between the waters which were good for gudgeon and those which preferred carp or roach; he knew the favourite banks for bream and the various baits which tempted different fish.

But while watching his float bobbing on the surface of the water, his mind was haunted by other visions.

He became friends with the head of the sub-prefect's office and the chief of the police; and they played whist in the evenings at the Café de Commerce but while his mournful eye was undressing the queen of clubs or the queen of diamonds, the problem of the missing legs in these figures quite confused the images hatching in his brain.

Then he thought of a plan, a really cunning Norman plan. He persuaded his wife to take a maid who suited her, not a pretty girl, a flirt or a dressy type but a strapping, stocky girl, whom he had carefully briefed and who would arouse no suspicions.

She was recommended to them in confidence by the tax inspector, a friend in the know and an accomplice who guaranteed her in every respect. Madame Bombard accepted with trust the treasure who was introduced to her.

Simon was happy, cautiously happy, fearful of unforeseen difficulties.

He only escaped the anxious surveillance of his wife for very brief moments here and there without peace.

He looked for a trick, a stratagem and finished by finding one that succeeded perfectly.

Madame Bombard, who had nothing to do, went to bed early, while Bombard who played whist at the Café de Commerce returned home each night at half past nine precisely. He arranged for Victorine to wait in the darkness in the corridor of the house, on the steps of the entrance hall. He had five minutes at the most because he always dreaded a surprise; but in the end from time to time five minutes was sufficient to satisfy his desire and, since he was generous with his pleasures, he slipped a louis into the hand of the servant who went back up to her attic very quickly.

He was laughing, he was triumphing all alone and like King Midas' barber[1] fishing for goldfish in the reeds of the river, he repeated out loud:

"Screwed up, the boss."

And the joy of screwing up Madame Bombard certainly made up for him for everything that was incomplete and imperfect in his conquest of convenience.

Then, one evening as usual he found Victorine waiting for him at the steps, but she seemed more lively, more animated than normal and he stayed perhaps ten minutes at the rendez-vous in the corridor.

When he entered the conjugal bedroom, Madame Bombard was not there. He felt a big cold shiver running down his spine and he fell into a chair tortured wit anxiety.

She re-appeared a candleholder in her hand.

Trembling, he asked:

"You have been out?"

Calmly, she replied:

"I have been in the kitchen to drink a glass of water."

He forced himself to play down the suspicions which she could have had. But she seemed quiet, happy, trusting; and he was re-assured.

The next day, when they went into the dining room for lunch and Victorine was putting the cutlets on the table, Madame Bombard rose and held out to her a louis which she held delicately between two fingers and she said in her calm and serious accent:

"Look, my girl, take the twenty-five francs which you were deprived of yesterday evening. I am handing them to you."

And the dumbfounded girl took the gold coin which she looked at stupidly, while Bombard, distraught, gaped at his wife with enormous eyes.

THE ROOM 11.

"What! You don't know why Judge Amandon was posted?"

"No, no idea."

"Needless to say, he never knew either. But it is a most odd story."

"Tell me about it."

"You must remember Madame Amandon, that pretty slim little brunette, so chic and smart. Everybody in Pertuis-le-Long used to call her Madame Marguerite."

"Yes, perfectly."

Well listen. You will recall also how she was respected and looked up to as the person the best loved of anyone in the town; she knew how to receive, organise a fête, a charity bazaar, find money for the poor, and entertain the young people in a thousand ways....

She was very elegant and a mighty flirt but with a platonic flirtatiousness and a delightful provincial elegance, for that little woman was provincial, an exquisite provincial.

The smart journalists who are all Parisian sing us the praises of the Parisian lady a thousand times because they only know her, but, personally, I maintain that the provincial is worth a hundred times more when she is upper class.

The stylish provincial has a quite special charm, more discreet than that of the Parisian, less showy; she promises nothing but gives a lot while the Parisian for most of the time promises a lot but gives nothing – in the bedroom.

With the Parisian, it is the elegant triumph and deceitful cheek. With the provincial, it is true modesty.

A smart little provincial lady, with her brisk bourgeois air, her deceptive local candour, her artless smile and her nice clever – but tenacious – little infatuations, must show a thousand times more cunning, flexibility and female wiles than all the Parisians put together in order to satisfy her tastes and peccadillos without arousing suspicion, gossip or scandal in a little town when all eyes are on her through every window.

Madame Amandon was a type of that rare breed but charming. One would never have suspected, never have thought that her life was not simple like her look, a sidelong look open and warm but so honest – go and see it!

So she had an admirable trick, a brilliant invention, marvellously ingenious and incredibly simple.

She picked all her lovers from the army and kept them for three years, the time of their posting in the garrison – so there you are – she did not have love, she had flair.

As soon as a new regiment arrived in Pertuis-le-Long, she took details of all the officers between thirty and forty years old – for below thirty one lacks tact and after forty one is often in decline.

Oh! She knew all the ranks as well as the colonel. She knew everything, everything, personal habits, training, education, physical qualities, resistance to fatigue, of patient or violent character, wealth, tendency to save or overspend. Then she made her choice. She had a preference for men with a calm temperament like her, but she wanted them to be handsome. Also she did not want them to have had any known liaison or love affair which could have left traces or might have caused some talk; a man whose affairs are talked about is never a man truly discreet.

Having identified the officer who would be her lover during the three years of the regulation posting, all that she now had to do was to give him the signal.

What about women who adopt the usual methods, the routes commonly followed, the courtship, all the stages of conquest and resistance, allowing one day a kiss on the fingers, the next day the wrist, the day after the cheek, then the mouth and then the rest, and, after all that discover that they are undecided.

She had a quicker method, more discreet and more sure. She gave a ball.

The selected officer invited the mistress of the house to dance; then during the waltz whirled around, exhilarated by the rapid movements, she clung to him closely, clasped his hand tightly continuously as to indicate that she was available.

If he did not get the message, he was only an idiot, and she passed on to number two in the portfolio of her prospects.

If he understood, the thing was done, without fuss, without compromising intrigues and without innumerable dates.

What could be simpler and more practical?

I wish that women would use a similar procedure to make us understand that they find us attractive! How easily that would put paid to difficulties, speeches, gestures, confusions and mis-understandings! How often we probably miss possible happiness, for who can penetrate the mysterious thinking, the secret impulses, the silent physical appeals, everything that is unknowable in the soul of a woman, whose tongue remains silent and whose eyes are pale and impenetrable?

As soon as he had got the message, he asked her for a date. She made him wait a month or six weeks, to spy on him, to find out more about him and to be on her guard in case he had some dangerous faults.

During this period, he racked his brain to decide where they would be able to meet without risk; he thought up difficult arrangements which were hardly foolproof.

Then, during some official reception, she said to him in a very low voice:

"On Tuesday evening go to The Golden Horse hotel near the ramparts on the Vouziers road and ask for Mademoiselle Clarisse. I will be expecting you and above all be in civilian clothes."

In fact for the last eight years she had rented annually a furnished room in this little known inn. It was the idea of her first lover, which she found practical, and, when he had gone, she kept the nest.

Oh! A second rate nest, four walls covered with light grey wallpaper with blue flowers, a pine bed behind muslin curtains, an armchair purchased to her order through the good offices of the innkeeper, a bedside rug and some vessels necessary for the toilet! What more was needed?

On the walls there were three large photographs. Three colonels on horseback; the colonels of her lovers. Why? Unable to keep their pictures as a direct souvenir, perhaps in this way she wished to retain their memories indirectly?

And you will ask whether she was ever recognised by anybody during all her visits to the Golden Horse?

Never! Nobody!

Her technique was admirable and simple. She used to plan and arrange a series of charity and religious meetings which she often used to attend but which sometimes she missed. Her husband who knew all about her charitable works which cost him mighty dear, had no suspicions.

So, once the assignation was arranged, she would say at dinner in front of the servants:

"I am going this evening to the Association for flannel waistbands for the aged paralytics."

And she went out about eight o'clock, dropped into the Association and left immediately. She passed through various streets and finding herself alone in some alleyway, in some dark corner without a street lamp, she took off her hat and replaced it with a maid's bonnet which she carried under her cloak; then she unfolded a white apron concealed in the same fashion and tied it round her waist; next she packed away her town hat and cloak which up to then had been covering her shoulders into a bag and trotted off boldly, her hips uncovered, a little housemaid on an errand; sometimes she even ran as if she was in a great hurry.

So who could have recognised in this slim and vivacious servant the wife of Judge Amandon?

She arrived at the Golden Horse and went straight up to her room since she already had the key; the fat proprietor, Master Trouveau, seeing her passing his desk, used to mutter:

"There you are, Mademoiselle Clarisse going to her lovers."

He might well have guessed something, the crafty fellow, but he was not looking to find out more and for sure he would have been really surprised to learn that his client was Madame Amandon or Madame Marguerite, as one used to say in Perthuis-le-Long.

But, here is how the horrible exposure took place.

*

Mademoiselle Clarisse never came to her assignations two evenings in succession, never, never. She was too smart and too prudent for that. Master Trouveau was well aware of it since not once in eight years had he seen her arriving for a visit two days in succession. Often during busy days he had even made her room available for a night.

But last summer in July when his Honour the Judge was away for a week, Madame was experiencing some passionate impulses. Since there was no fear of being surprised, she asked her lover, the handsome Commander Varangelles one Tuesday evening while they were parting whether he would like to se her again the next day. He replied:

"But, of course!"

And it was agreed that they would meet up at the normal time on Wednesday. She said in a low voice:

"Darling, if you are the first to arrive, you will get into bed and wait for me."

They kissed and separated.

But next day about ten o'clock when Master Trouveau was reading the Pertuis News, the town's republican journal, he shouted across to his wife who was plucking a chicken in the yard:

"Look at this. Cholera in the district. A man died yesterday at Vauvigny."

Then he thought no more about it; his hotel was fully booked and business was going very nicely.

Towards midday, a traveller arrived, a sort of tourist; he drank two absinthes and sat down to a good lunch; and since it was very hot, he absorbed a litre of wine and at least two litres of water.

Next he took his coffee and his liqueur or rather three liqueurs. Then, feeling a little bloated, he requested a room to sleep an hour or two. As there was no longer a single room free, the proprietor, having consulted his wife, gave him Mademoiselle Clarisse's room.

The man went upstairs and then around five o'clock, since he had not been seen leaving, the proprietor went to wake him!

What a surprise, he was dead!

The innkeeper went downstairs to find his wife:

"What do you say, the character I put in the room 11, I really think he is dead."

She raised her arms:

"Not possible! Lord God, is it cholera?"

Master Trouveau shook his head:

"I would rather think that it is apoplexy; he is as black as wine dregs."

But his good lady was alarmed and kept on repeating:

"We must not talk about it, we must not talk about it. People will think that it is cholera. Go and report it but don't talk. They will take him away during the night to avoid being seen, neither seen nor known. I implore you."

The man murmured:

"Mademoiselle Clarisse was here yesterday. The room is free this evening."

Then he went to look for the doctor who certified the death from a stroke after a heavy meal. It was agreed with the police commissioner that the body would be removed around midnight, so that nothing would be suspected in the hotel.

*

It was scarcely nine o'clock when Madame Amandon furtively slipped up the stairs in the Golden Horse without being seen by anybody on that day. She reached her room, opened the door and went in. A candle was burning on the mantelpiece. She turned towards the bed. The commandant was lying down with the curtains drawn.

She announced:

"One minute, darling, I am coming."

She then undressed with feverish speed, throwing her boots on the floor and her corset on the armchair. Next her black dress and her petticoats fell in a circle round her and she stood up in red silk underwear like a flower which had just bloomed.

As the commandant still had not uttered a word, she asked:

"Are you asleep, big boy?"

There was no reply and she started to laugh, muttering:

"Look, he is asleep, it is too funny!"

She had kept on her stockings of black silk, and running to the bed she slipped into it quickly, at the same time throwing her arms round him and kissing him full on the lips to wake him suddenly – the icy corpse of the tourist!

For a second, she remained motionless, too terrified to comprehend anything. The coldness of that lifeless flesh had inflicted on her body a dreadful and mindless horror before her brain could even begin to reflect.

She leapt out of the bed shaking from head to foot; then, running to the mantelpiece, she grabbed the candle, came back and looked! She saw a frightful face which she did not recognise, black, swollen, eyes closed, and the jaw in a horrible grimace.

She let out a scream, one of those high pitched screams which women make in a panic, and dropping the candle, she opened the door and fled naked into the corridor continuing to shriek in a dreadful fashion.

A travelling salesman in socks, who was in Room Number 4 came immediately and received her into his arms.

Alarmed, he asked:

"What is it, dear child?"

She stammered wildly:

"Some …. someone …. has been killed in my room."

Other travellers appeared. The proprietor himself ran up.

Then, suddenly, the commandant revealed his tall figure at the end of the corridor.

As soon as she saw him, she rushed towards him, screaming:

"Save me, save me Gontran …. Somebody has been killed in our room."

Explanations were difficult. However Monsieur Trouveau told the truth and since he could vouch for Mademoiselle Clarisse, he asked that she should be released immediately. But the travelling salesman in socks, having examined the body, claimed that a crime had been committed and he persuaded the other guests to prevent the departure of Mademoiselle Clarisse and her lover.

They hung around to await the arrival of the Commissioner of Police who gave them their freedom but was not discreet.

The following month His Honour Judge Amandon received a promotion with a new residence.

THE CUPBOARD

We were talking after dinner about prostitutes, what else is there for men to talk about?

One of us said:

"Listen, a funny thing happened to me once on this subject."

And he told the story:

One evening last winter, I was suddenly taken with one of those distressing and oppressive fits of listlessness which from time to time gets hold of one, body and soul. I was alone at home and I really felt that if I stayed like that I was going to have a terrible attack of depression, one of those attacks which must lead to suicide when they are frequent.

I put on my overcoat and went out without knowing in the slightest what I was going to do. Having gone down as far as the boulevards, I started to wander along the cafés which were almost empty because it was raining; it was a thin rain which was falling, a rain which damps the spirits as much as the clothes, not one of those heavy showers beating down in torrents and sending breathless passers-by scampering into taxis; it was not a rain which is so fine, that you did not feel the drops, but one of those wet rains whose droplets fall on you incessantly and imperceptibly and soon covers your clothes with a film of icy, penetrating water.

What to do? I went up and down trying to kill a couple of hours and discovering for the first time that in Paris in the evening there was no place to relax. Finally I decided to go to the Folies-Bergère, [1] that amusements hall for prostitutes.

There was hardly any one in the grand room. The long horseshoe shaped walkway contained only individuals of little importance whose common breeding was shown up by their attitude, by their clothing and their hats, by the cut of their beard and their hair, and by their complexion. It was with difficulty that one might occasionally pick out a man who one might reckon to have washed, properly, and whose general dress was wholly correct. As for the girls, always the same, awful girls that you know, ugly, tired, drooping and going on the hunt with that imbecile look of contempt which they take on, I do not know why.

I was saying to myself that none of these shapeless creatures, greasy rather than fat, puffed up here, skinny there, with bellies like barrels and with knock-kneed legs like wading birds – none of them worth the single louis they obtained with great difficulty after having asked for five.

But suddenly I spotted a small one who seemed nice to me, not that young, but fresh, cheeky and provocative. I stopped her and stupidly without thinking made my bargain for the night. I did not want to return home alone, all alone. I much preferred the company and embrace of this small girl.

Then I followed her. She lived in a big, big house, Martyrs street. The gas lights were already out on the stairs. I went up slowly striking a match light from time to time, stumbling against the steps and none too happy behind the rustle of the skirts I could hear in front of me.

She stopped at the fourth floor and having relocked the outside door, she asked:

"So you are staying until to-morrow?"

"But yes. You know very well that is what we agreed."

"That's all right, darling, it was only that I wanted to know. Wait for me a moment, I will return in a minute."

And she left me in the darkness. I heard her shutting two doors, then it appeared that she was speaking to someone. I was surprised and anxious; the thought of a pimp crossed my mind. But I had fists and a strong back "we'll see" I thought.

I listened attentively all ears. Someone was stirring, moving gently with every precaution. Then another door was opened and I thought that I was again hearing someone speaking but quite low.

She came back, carrying a lighted candle:

"You can come in," she said.

She used the familiar form of address. It was a sign of possession. I went in and having crossed the dining room where it was obvious that no-one ever took meals, I entered a typical prostitute's bedroom, the furnished bedroom, with serge curtains and a bright red silk eiderdown spotted with suspect stains.

She continued:

"Make yourself at home, darling."

I inspected the apartment suspiciously. However nothing seemed worrying.

She got undressed so quickly that she was in bed before I had taken off my overcoat. She started to laugh:

"So, what is the matter? Have you changed into a statue? Look, hurry up!"

I followed her example and joined her.

Five minutes later I had the mad urge to get dressed again and leave. But that depressing listlessness which had overcome me at home, kept me back, taking away from me every inclination to stir, and I stayed there despite the disgust I felt in that public bed. The sensual charm which I believed I had seen in this creature under the lights of the theatre hall had disappeared and now between my arms, lying against me flesh to flesh, I had nothing more than a common prostitute, same as them all, whose indifferent and complacent kiss had an after taste of garlic.

I started to talk to her.

"Have you been living here long?" I said.

"Actually for the past six months – from 15th January."

"Where were you before that?"

"I was in Clauzel street but the concierge gave me a bad time and I gave in my notice."

Then she started on an interminable story of the doorkeeper who had spread gossip about her.

But suddenly I heard something stirring quite close to us. At first it had been a sigh, then a slight noise as if someone was turning over in a chair.

I sat up abruptly in the bed and asked:

"What was that noise there?"

She calmly reassured me:

"Do not worry, darling, it is the neighbour. The partition is so thin that one hears everything as if it was here. These filthy premises, look, they are a cardboard box."

Such was my laziness that I sank back again under the sheets and we started to chat again. I was pestered by that stupid curiosity which pushes all men to question these creatures about their first experience, to lift the veil on the first lapse, to find in them a remote trace of innocence, perhaps to love them; possibly there might be a genuine word to bring back a quick memory of their past decency and honesty; so I pressed her with questions on her first lovers.

I knew she would lie. What did it matter? Amongst all those lies, perhaps I would find something sincere and touching.

"Let's see," I said, "who was it?"

"It was a rowing man, darling."

"Ah! Tell me. 'Where were you?"

"I was at Argenteuil."

"What were you doing there?"

"I was a maid in an inn."

"Which inn?"

"At the 'Marin d'eau douce'."

"Good God! With Bonanfan."

"Yes, that's right."

"And how did he court you, this oarsman?"

"While I was making his bed. He forced me."

But suddenly I remembered the theory of one of my doctor friends, a medical researcher and scientist, whose continuous service in a big hospital put him in daily contact with unmarried mothers and common prostitutes, with all the miseries of women, poor women who had become the hideous prey of the wandering male with money in his pocket.

'Always', he used to tell me, 'always a girl is violated by a man of her class and social condition. I have volumes of evidence on that. The rich classes are accused of plucking the flower of innocence from the children of the people. It is not true. The rich pay for the bouquet which has already been picked! They also pick but it is the second flowering. They never cut the first'.

Then turning towards my companion, I started to laugh:

You realise that I know it, your story. It was not the oarsman who was the first to have you."

"Oh! Yes darling, I swear it was."

"You are lying, darling."

"Oh! No, I promise you!"

"You are lying. Come on, tell me everything."

She was astonished and seemed to hesitate.

I went on:

"My sweet child, I am a magician and a hypnotist. If you do not tell me the truth, I will put you to sleep and then I will know it."

She was frightened, being stupid like all of them. She stammered:

"How did you guess?"

I continued:

"Come on. Talk."

"Oh! The first time that was practically nothing. It was a holiday in the country. An extra chef was brought in, M. Alexandre. As soon as he arrived, he did exactly as he pleased. He gave orders to everyone, the landlord, the landlord's wife, as if he was a king. He was a big, handsome man who did not keep to his place behind his stove. He was always shouting: 'Come on, some butter – some eggs – some madeira'. And I had to bring that to him straightaway on the run, otherwise he became angry and he used to tell you about it in such a way as to make you blush under your skirts.

When the day was finished, he began to smoke his pipe in front of the door. And as I brushed past him with a pile of plates, he says to me like this: 'Let's go kid, come and show me the countryside on the riverbank'? Me, like an idiot, I went; and we had hardly been on the bank when he had me so quick that I did not even know what he was doing. Then he left by the nine o'clock train. I haven't seen him since."

I asked:

"Is that all?"

She stammered:

"Oh! I really think that Florentin is his!"

"Who is Florentin?"

"He is my little one."

"Ah! Very nice. And you made the rowing man believe that he was the father, didn't you?"

"So what?"

"He had money, the oarsman."

"Yes, he left me an income of three hundred francs for Florentin."

I was beginning to enjoy myself. I went on:

"Very good, my girl, that's very good. You are really a lot less stupid than I thought. And how old is Florentin now?"

She replied:

"He is twelve; he will take his first communion in the spring."

"That's perfect, and ever since you carry out your trade with a clear conscience."

"One does what one can….."

Then a loud noise coming from the room itself made me jump out of bed with a bound; it was the noise of a body falling and getting up with hands groping for a wall.

I had grabbed the candle and was looking around me, alarmed and furious. She had risen as well and was trying to hold me back and restrain me, muttering:

"It was nothing, darling, I assure you it was nothing."

But I had discovered from which side the strange noise came. I went straight to a door concealed at the head of our bed and abruptly I opened it ….. I saw a thin and pale small boy, trembling and staring at me, wide eyed and in a panic; he was sitting beside a big wicker chair from which he had just fallen.

As soon as he saw me, he started to cry and throwing his arms round his mother:

"It's not my fault, mum, it's not my fault. I was asleep and I fell. You mustn't tell me off. It's not my fault."

I turned round to the woman and declared:

"What does this mean?"

She seemed confused and sorry. She said in a strange voice:

"What do you want? I don't earn enough myself to board him out! I need to take care of him and I do not have the wherewithal to pay for another room, damn it! He sleeps with me when I have nobody. When someone comes for an hour or two, he can easily stay in the cupboard, he can keep quiet. He knows that. But when someone stays the whole night, like you, it is tiring for his back to sleep in a chair, that child ….. it's not his fault, not at all …..I would really like to see you ….. sleeping all night on a chair …..you would tell me all about it…."

She was becoming animated and angry and was shouting.

The child continued to cry. A poor, timid, puny child, yes, truly a child from the cupboard, the cupboard which was cold and dark, the child who comes out from time to time to reclaim a little warmth in the bed when it was temporarily empty.

As for me, I also had the urge to cry.

And I returned to sleep at home.

ROGER'S METHOD

I was walking on the boulevard with Roger when some salesman or other shouted at us:

"Need a method of getting rid of your mother-in-law! Ask!"

I stopped dead and said to my comrade:

"There is a cry which reminds me of a question which I have been meaning to put to you for a long time; so what is this 'Roger's method' of which your wife is always speaking. She jokes about that in such a funny and knowing fashion that as far as I am concerned it must be a question of some aphrodisiac potion of which you would have the secret. Every time that one mentions in her presence a young man who is tired, exhausted and out of breath, she turns towards you laughing and says:

"You need to indicate to him Roger's method." "And the oddest thing in this whole matter is that you blush every time."

Roger replied:

There is something in it, and if my wife suspected that there was some truth in what she is saying, I assure you that she would shut up... I am going to tell you the story personally in confidence. You know that I married a widow with whom I was very much in love. My wife has always been free in her speech and before becoming my legal companion, we often used to have some spicy conversations, incidentally quite acceptable amongst widows who have kept the taste of spice in their mouths. She very much used to love amusing stories and coarse jokes – without any underhand motives. In certain cases, slips of the tongue are not serious; she is slightly indecent while I am a little shy and frequently, before our marriage, she used to enjoy embarrassing me with questions and jokes to which I did not find it easy to reply. Besides, perhaps it was this forward-ness of hers which made me fall in love with her. As regards being in love, I was head over heels, body and soul, and she knew it, the so-and-so.

We decided that there would be no formalities and no honeymoon. After blessing in church, we would offer a collation to our witnesses, then we would go for a ride tête-à-tête in a carriage and we would come back for dinner at my place – Helder street.

So, our witnesses having left, there we were climbing into the carriage; I said to the coachman to take us to the Bois de Boulogne. It was the end of June and marvellous weather.

As soon as we were alone, she started to laugh.

"Dear Roger," she said, "now is the time to be romantic. Let's see how you are going to take to it."

Called to order in this way, I was immediately paralysed. I kissed her hand, I repeated: "I love you". Twice I was bold enough to kiss her neck but I was embarrassed by the passers-by. Continuously she repeated in a funny provocative little way: "And now ….. and now…" This 'and now' got on my nerves and depressed me. One couldn't do it in broad daylight in a carriage in the Bois de Boulogne…. you understand.

She appreciated my embarrassment and was enjoying herself. From time to time she repeated:

"I really am afraid that I am going to be badly let down. You are giving me plenty to worry about."

Also, personally, I was beginning to have worries myself. When I am inhibited, I am no longer capable of anything.

At dinner she was charming. And to give myself confidence, I dismissed my servant who was embarrassing me. Oh! We were behaving correctly, but you know how silly people become when they are amorous; we drink from the same glass, we eat off the same plate, with the same fork; we enjoy munching biscuits from both ends so that our lips meet in the middle.

She said to me:

"I would like a little champagne."

I had forgotten that bottle on the sideboard. I took it, tore off the wire and pressed at the cork to open it. It did not pop; Gabrielle began to smile and murmured:

"Bad sign."

I pushed the swollen cork with my thumb, levering it to the left and to the right and suddenly I broke it at the level of the neck.

Gabrielle sighed:

"My poor Roger."

I got a corkscrew and twisted it into what remained of the cork in the neck. Then I found it impossible to withdraw it! I had to call for Prosper. Now my wife was laughing uproariously and was repeating:

"Ah well ….. ah well ….. I see that I can count on you."

She was half tight.

She was three quarters tight after the coffee.

In going to bed, a widow does not require all the motherly formalities necessary for a young girl; Gabrielle went quietly into her bedroom, saying to me:

"Smoke your cigar for a quarter of an hour."

When I rejoined her, I admit that I lacked confidence in myself. I felt nervous, bothered, ill at ease.

I took my place as her husband. She said nothing. She looked at me with a smile on her lips and the obvious urge to make fun of me. This sarcasm, at a time like this, succeeded in disconcerting me and, I admit it, it turned me off all together – arms and legs.

When Gabrielle noted my … embarrassment, she did nothing to reassure me, quite the contrary. She asked me with a little indifferent air:

"Do you have as much energy every day?"

I could not stop myself answering:

"Listen, you are intolerable."

Then she began to laugh again in an excessive, disagreeable and annoying manner.

It is true that I made a sorry sight and that I must have had a right stupid look.

From time to time between mad bursts of mirth, choking, she declared:

"Go on …… courage ….. a little energy … my … my poor friend."

Then she carried on laughing so wildly that she was breaking into screams.

In the end I felt so irritated, so furious with myself and her that I realised that I was going to slap her if I did not leave the place.

I jumped out of bed and dressed swiftly and angrily, without saying a word.

Suddenly she calmed down, and understanding that I was angry, she asked:

"What are you doing? Where are you going?"

I did not reply. I went down into the street. I felt like killing someone, to take revenge, to commit some folly. I went straight ahead at a fast walk and abruptly I had the idea of going to a brothel.

Who knows? It would be a test, an experience and perhaps an education? In any case it would be a vengeance! And if ever I might be sometime deceived by my wife, always she would have been deceived by me first.

I did not hesitate. I knew an establishment not far from my residence; I ran there and entered like people do who throw themselves into the water to see if they still know how to swim.

I swam all right and very well. And I stayed there a long time, savouring this secret and subtle revenge. Then I found myself again in the street at that cool hour just when night is about to finish. Now I felt calm and sure of myself, happy, at ease and ready again, it seemed, for exploits.

Next, slowly I went back home and gently opened the bedroom door.

Gabrielle was reading, propped up on her pillow. She raised her head and asked in a timid tone of voice:

"So there you are? What has been the matter with you?"

I did not reply. I undressed with confidence and recovered, as the triumphant master, the place I had left as a fugitive.

She was amazed and convinced that I had made use of some mysterious secret.

And now constantly she speaks of Roger's method as if she was referring to some infallible scientific process.

But alas! Here we are ten years from then and to-day the same test would no longer have much chance of success, at least for me.

But if you have a friend who dreads his emotion on his wedding night, tell him of my stratagem but assure him that from twenty to thirty five years it is not the best manner of untangling the knots – as the sire of Brantome[1] would have said.

A FAILURE

On the way to Turin I went through Corsica.

At Nice I took the boat for Bastia; as soon as we were at sea, I noticed a young woman sitting on the deck; she was looking into the distance and seemed to be nice and quite shy. I said to myself:

"Ah, here is my crossing."

I settled myself opposite her, and while looking at her, I asked myself all those questions one should ask when one comes across a young woman who interests you; her social position, her age, her character. Then you make a guess by what you can see and by what you don't see. With your eye and your imagination you probe the interior of her blouse and underneath her dress. You note the size of the bust when she is sitting down; you try to spot the ankle; you notice the quality of the hand which will indicate the fineness of the wrists and ankles, also the quality of the ear which will point to her origins better than a birth certificate which is always disputable. You try hard to listen to her speaking to assess her intelligence and by the tone of her voice the inclinations of her heart. For the inflexion and nuances of speech reveal to an experienced observer the mysterious composition of an intellect; there is always a perfect harmony between the thought itself and the organ which expresses it, although difficult to recognise.

So I was observing my neighbour closely, looking for signs, analysing gestures, and waiting for examples of her likely behaviour.

She opened a little bag and pulled out a newspaper. I was rubbing my hands and saying to myself: "Tell me what you are reading, I will tell you what you are thinking."

She started with an article on the front page which she was reading avidly and with enjoyment. The title of the journal leapt to my eye: 'The Echo of Paris'[1]. I was baffled. She was reading a piece by Scholl. Damn! She was a Scholliste – a Scholliste? She started to smile; a sense of fun. But not prudish, good girl. Very well. A Scholliste – yes, that means that she's fond of the French character, the fineness, the salt, even the pepper. Good point. I was thinking: "Let's see and check."

I went and sat down next to her and just as attentively I started to read a volume of poetry which I had brought when I left: 'La Chanson d'Amour" by Felix Frank[2]. I noticed that with a quick glance she had picked up the title on the cover like a bird who picks at a fly in the air. Several passengers went past in front of us to look at her. But she seemed only to be concentrating on her article. When she had finished it, she put the paper down between us.

I greeted her and said:

"Will you let me, Madame, have a glance at your paper?"

"Certainly, sir."

"Perhaps in the meantime I can offer you this volume of verse?"

"Certainly, sir. Is it amusing?"

I was a little upset by this question. One does not ask if a collection of verse is amusing. I replied:

"It is better than that. It is charming, delicate and very beautiful."

"Then, let me see it."

She took the book, opened it and started to thumb through it with a slightly surprised air proving that she did not often read verse.

Sometimes she seemed touched, sometimes she smiled, but with a different sort of smile than when she was reading her paper.

Suddenly I asked her:

"Are you enjoying that?"

"Yes, but personally I like something cheerful, very cheerful, I am not sentimental."

Then we started to chat. I learned that she was the wife of a captain in the Dragoons garrisoned at Ajaccio and that she was on her way to rejoin her husband.

In a few minutes, I guessed that she hardly loved him, this husband! She loved him, yes, but with reservations like one might love a man who has not totally fulfilled the expectations aroused during the days of the engagement. He had taken her from garrison to garrison, to a multitude of small towns, gloomy and so unexciting! Now he was sending for her to come to this island, which had to be dismal. No, life was not enjoyable for everybody. She still would have preferred to live with her parents at Lyon because she knew everyone at Lyon. But now she had to go to Corsica. Really the minister was not being kind to her husband considering that he had a very good service record.

Then we spoke of places where she might prefer to live.

I asked:

"Do you like Paris?"

"Oh! sir, do I like Paris! Can there be such a question?" And she started to talk to me about Paris with such keenness and enthusiasm and with such a frenzy of longing that I was thinking: "There you are, there is the tune I must play."

She adored Paris from afar, with the fury of suppressed hunger, with the exasperated passion of the provincial, with the flustered impatience of a caged bird that sees a wood all day long from behind the bars where it is trapped.

She started to question me stammering in her anxiety; she wanted to know everything all in five minutes. She was familiar with the names of all the celebrated people and still plenty of others I had never heard of.

"How is M. Gounod? And M. Sardou? Oh! Sir, how I love M. Sardou's plays! He is so light-hearted and so witty! Each time I see one I am in a dream for a week! I've also read a book by M. Daudet which I enjoyed very much! Sapho, do you know it? Is he a nice fellow, M. Daudet? Have you seen him? And M. Zola, how is he? If you knew how 'Germinal' made me cry! You recall the small child who dies under ground. How terrible it is! I was nearly ill. Honestly it is not something to laugh at! I have also read M. Bourget's 'Cruelle Enigme'! I have a cousin who lost the plot of that novel so totally that she wrote to M Bourget. Personally I found it too romantic. I prefer something humorous. Do you know M. Grevin? And M. Coquelin? And M.Damala? And M. Rochefort? They say that he has so much atmosphere! And M. de Cassagnac? Apparently he fights every day?"[3]

*

At the end of about an hour her questions began to dry up, and having satisfied her curiosity in my most imaginative way, it was my turn to speak.

I told her stories of society, Parisian society, high society. She listened all ears and all heart. Oh! For sure, she must have received a very good idea of the beautiful and distinguished ladies of Paris. They were merely about romantic exploits, meetings, swift victories and passionate defeats. From time to time she asked me:

"Oh! Is it like that, high society?"

I smiled mischievously:

"Good God, it is only the minor bourgeoisie who lead a boring and monotonous life out of respect for morality, a morality which is to nobody's liking."

Then I started to undermine morality with large helpings of sarcasm, philosophy and plenty of jokes. Then in an offhand manner I mocked the poor creatures who allowed themselves to grow old without knowing anything of the satisfaction, of the sweetness of romance and affection, without having savoured the delicious pleasure of stolen kisses which are deep and passionate; and that was because they had married a big chump of a husband whose conjugal dignity allows them to go right to their death bed in ignorance of every sophisticated sensuality and every refined sentiment.

Then again I quoted stories, anecdotes, secret love affairs, which I maintained were known to the whole world. Also, as a refrain, it was always the subtle and discreet eulogy of quick and secret passion, of the sensation stolen in passing like a fruit and forgotten as soon as experienced.

Night fell, a calm and warm night. The big ship, its engines throbbing, slid through the sea under the immense ceiling of the purple and starry sky.

The small woman said nothing more. She was breathing slowly and sometimes sighing. Suddenly she got up:

"I am going to bed," she said, "good night, sir."

And she shook my hand.

I knew that on the next evening she was due to take the coach from Bastia to Ajaccio, a journey which took all night.

I replied:

"Good night, Madame."

Then in my turn I retired to the bunk in my cabin.

From the morning of the following day, I had booked the three seats on a carriage, all three for me alone.

As I climbed into the ancient vehicle which was going to leave Bastia at nightfall, the driver asked me if I would give up a corner to a lady.

Quickly I asked:

"To which lady?"

"An officer's wife going to Ajaccio."

"Tell the lady that I will gladly offer her a place."

She arrived, having spent the day asleep, she said. She apologised, thanked me and climbed in.

The carriage was a sort of hermetically sealed box; there were only two doors to let in the daylight. So here we were tête-à-tête inside. We set off at a trot and then a fast trot, before tackling the road through the mountains. A fresh and strong scent of fragrant plants came in through the lowered windows, that penetrating odour which Corsica gives off so far that sailors recognise it offshore, a pervasive smell like that of a body, like the whiff of green vegetation extracted by the fierce sun and evaporating in the passing breeze.

Again I started to talk about Paris and again she began to listen to me with feverish attention. My tales became risqué, shrewdly revealing, full of veiled and dangerous words, words which make the blood run.

Night had fallen completely. I could no longer see anything not even the white patch which just before had been the face of the young woman. It was only the coachman's lamp that lit up the four horses that were climbing at a walking pace.

Sometimes we could hear the noise of a stream rushing over rocks and mingled with the sound of the horses' bells, a noise that was then soon lost in the distance behind us.

Gently I moved my foot to touch hers, which she did not withdraw. Then I waited without moving and suddenly, changing tack, I was talking of love and affection. I had put out my hand to hold hers which she showed no sign of withdrawing. All the time I was whispering close to her ear and quite near her mouth. I could already feel her heart beating against my chest. Certainly it was beating fast and strongly – a good sign; – then slowly I kissed her neck, convinced that I had got her, and I was so sure that she wanted it that I would have put money on it.

But suddenly as if she was just waking up, she gave a jolt, such a jolt that I went crashing to the other end of the carriage. Then before I could realise what was happening, reflect and think of anything, first all I received five or six violent slaps, then a hail of short, sharp punches, hitting me everywhere and in such a way that I was unable to parry them in the complete darkness which enveloped this struggle.

I stretched out my hands desperately trying to grab her arms. Then, not knowing what to do, abruptly I turned my back to her furious attack and buried my head in a corner of the upholstery.

Perhaps from the sound of the blows, apparently she understood this hopeless manoeuvre and she quickly stopped hitting me.

After a few seconds she regained her corner and started to cry with big, wild sobs which went on for about an hour.

I resumed my seat, very upset and ashamed. I would like to have said something but what could I say? I couldn't think of anything! Apologise? That would have been silly! What would you have said, you! Go on, admit it, nothing more!

Now she was snivelling and occasionally let out great sighs which touched me and made me feel sorry. I wanted to console her, hug her like one hugs tearful children, beg her pardon, go down on my hands and knees. But I did not dare.

They are really stupid these sorts of situations!

At last she calmed down, and we stayed in our respective corners, both of us motionless and dumb, while the carriage continued on its way, sometimes halting to change horses. On those occasions we both closed our eyes quickly so that no-one would disturb us, when the bright gleam of the stable lantern shone into the carriage. Then we set off again; and always the sweetly smelling and appetising air of the Corsican mountains caressed our lips and cheeks and intoxicated me like wine.

Christ, what a good trip ….. if my companion had been less silly!

But the daylight was slowly slipping into the carriage, the pale light of the first dawn. I looked at my neighbour. She appeared to be asleep. Next the sun rising behind the mountains was soon bathing an immense blue gulf with light, a gulf surrounded by enormous hills with granite peaks. At the edge of the gulf, a whitewashed town, still in the shadow, appeared before our eyes.

My neighbour now appeared to be waking up. She opened her eyes, (they were red), she opened her mouth to yawn as if she had been asleep a long time. Then she hesitated, blushed and stammered:

"Will we be arriving soon?"

"Yes, Madame, in scarcely an hour."

She continued, looking into the distance:

"It is very tiring, spending a night on a coach."

"Oh! Yes, it gives one a sore back."

"Especially after a sea crossing."

"Oh! Yes."

"Is that Ajaccio ahead?"

"Yes, Madame."

"I really would like to get there."

"I understand that."

The sound of her voice was a little strained, her bearing a little embarrassed, her eye a little furtive. Yet she seemed to have forgotten everything.

How unscrupulous their instincts were, these types! What diplomats! I admired her.

In fact after an hour we had arrived; a large dragoon of herculean dimensions was standing in front of the terminus; when he saw the carriage, he waived a handkerchief.

My neighbour jumped out and ran into his arms; she kissed him at least twenty times, repeating:

"Are you well? How I have hurried to see you again!"

My suitcase was brought down from the carriage and as I was discreetly retiring, she shouted to me:

"Oh! Sir you are going off without saying goodbye."

"Madame, I was leaving you to your happiness."

Then she said to her husband:

"Darling, thank the gentleman. He has been charming to me throughout the trip. He even offered me a place in his carriage which he had booked all for himself. We are so lucky to have such pleasant companions.

She husband shook my hand, thanking me heartily.

The young woman was smiling, watching us...... Me, personally I must have had a right stupid look!

SAVED

I

She came in like a bullet crashing through a window pane, the little marquise de Renedon; then before uttering a word she began to laugh, to laugh until tears came into her eyes, just like she had dome a month earlier while announcing to her friend that she had been unfaithful to the marquis out of revenge and only out of revenge and only the once because he was really too stupid and jealous.

The little baroness de Grangerie had thrown down the book she was reading on to the sofa and was looking at Annette with curiosity while already laughing herself.

Finally she asked:

'What is it you have done now?'

Oh! …. My dear …. It is too funny … too funny … can you imagine … I am saved! … Saved! … Saved!

What do you mean – saved?

Yes, saved!

From what?

From my husband, my dear, saved! Released! Free! Free! Free!

How do you mean – free? In what way?

In what way? Divorce! Yes, divorce! I have my divorce!

You are divorced?

No, not yet, silly! You can't get a divorce in three hours! But I have the evidence …. The evidence …. That he is unfaithful….. Think of it! … Red handed …. I have got him….

Oh! Tell me about it! So he was deceiving you?

Yes … that is to say no …. Yes and no … I don't know. The essential thing is that at last I have the evidence.

How have you done that?

How I have done it? I'll tell you! Oh! I've been hard, really hard. For three months now he has become hateful, quite hateful, brutal, despotic, finally revolting. I said to myself: This cannot last, I need a divorce! But how? That was not easy. I tried to get him to hit me. He didn't want to. He upset me from morning to night, he forced me to go out when I didn't want to, and to stay at home when I wished to dine in town; he made life unbearable from one end of the week to the other but he did not hit me.

Then I tried to find out if he had a mistress. Yes, he had one, but when he went to her place, he took a thousand precautions. Together they were impregnable. So guess what I did?

I cannot think.

Oh! You would never guess! I begged my brother to procure me a photograph of the tart.

Your husband's mistress?

Yes, That cost Jacques fifteen louis, the price of an evening from seven o'clock to midnight including dinner, three louis an hour. To cap it all he got the photograph.

It seems to me that he would have got it for less by adopting some ruse or other and without ….. without …. Without being obliged to go for the real thing at the same time.

Oh! She is pretty. That did not displease Jacques. And from my point of view I needed details on her, physical details, size, bust, complexion, well a thousand things.

I don't understand.

You will see. When I knew everything I wanted to know, I made an appointment … how shall I put it … with a business-man …. You know …. One of those men who deal in all kinds of business … of every type … agents … publicity … intelligence … well, you understand.

Yes, a little. And you told him?

I showed him the photograph of Clarisse (she was called Clarisse) and said to him: "I need a personal maid, who resembles this one. I want her to be pretty, elegant, slim and correct. I will pay her what is necessary. If that costs me three thousand francs, too bad. I will not need her for more than three months."

He looked very astonished, that man. He asked: "Does Madame wish her to be beyond reproach?"

I blushed and stammered: "But yes as regards honesty."

He continued: "And as for morals…" I did not dare reply. I merely gave an indication with my head which meant: "No." Then suddenly I realised that he had a horrible suspicion and losing my composure, I blurted out: "Oh! Sir ….. it is for my husband who is unfaithful to me … who is deceiving me in the town ….. and I want …I want him to deceive me at home … you understand … to surprise him…."

The man started to laugh and I understood from his look that he had given me his approval. Even he was finding me very hard. I could well have taken a bet that at that moment he felt like shaking my hand.

He told me: "In eight days, Madame, I will have your problem in hand and if necessary we will change the individual. I deal in results. You will only pay me after success. So this photograph is of your husband's mistress?"

"Yes, sir."

"A beautiful person who looks slimmer than she actually is. And what is the perfume?"

I did not understand: "How do you mean – what perfume?"

He smiled: "Yes, Madame, perfume is essential to seduce a man; for that gives him subconscious reminders which will put him in a position to act. Perfume establishes a vague confusion in his mind, troubles him and in reminding him of his pleasures, irritates him. It will also be necessary to try and find out what your husband was accustomed to eating while having dinner with that lady. You can serve him the same dishes on the evening when we are going to catch him. Oh! We'll get him, Madame, we'll get him."

I went away delighted. I had really fallen in with a very intelligent man.

II

Three days later I saw a tall girl arriving at home, brunette, very beautiful, with a modest attitude and at the same time firm and with a particularly unscrupulous look. With me she was very reasonable. As I did not know too much about her, I addressed her as mademoiselle; then she said to me: "Oh! Madame can call me Rose for short." We began to chat.

"Very well, Rose, you know why you are here?"

"Obviously, Madame"

"Very good, my girl …. And that … does not bother you too much?"

"Oh! Madame, it is the eighth divorce I've done; I am used to it."

"Then, that's perfect. Do you need a long time to succeed?"

"Oh! Madame, that all depends on monsieur's temperament. When I have seen monsieur tête-à-tête for five minutes, I will be able to give Madame a precise answer."

"You will se him presently, my child. But I am warning you that he is not handsome."

"That doesn't matter, Madame. I have already done separations from ugly gentlemen. But I will ask Madame, if she has been informed of the perfume?"

"Yes, my good Rose, – vervain."

"So much the better, Madame, I like that scent very much! Can Madame also tell me if monsieur's mistress wears silk underwear?"

"No, my child: it is very fine linen with lace."

"Oh! So she is a very correct person. Silk underwear is beginning to become common."

"What you say there is very true."

"Very well, Madame, I am going to take up my duties."

In fact she took up her duties immediately as if she had done nothing else all her life.

One hour later my husband returned. Rose did not even raise her eyes to him, but he raised his eyes to her all right. She was already smelling strongly of vervain. After five minutes she left.

Immediately he asked me:

"Who is that girl there?"

"But …. My new maid."

"Where did you find her?"

"It was baroness de Grangerie who passed her on to me with the very best references."

"Ah! She is pretty enough!"

"You think so?"

"But yes … for a lady's maid."

I was delighted. I felt that he was already nibbling.

The same evening Rose said to me: "I can now promise Madame that it will not take more than fifteen days. Monsieur is very easy!"

"Ah! You have already tried?"

"No, Madame, but that is obvious from the first glance. Already he has had the urge to kiss me while passing close to me."

"He has said nothing to you?"

"No, Madame; he has merely asked my name …. to hear the sound of my voice."

"Excellent, my good Rose. Go as fast as you can."

"Madame has nothing to fear. I will only put him off for as long as is necessary so as not to undervalue myself."

After the end of eight days my husband hardly went out at all. I used to see him all afternoon pacing up and down through the house; and what was more significant from his point of view, was that he did not stop me going out. And as far as I was concerned I was out all day ….. to … to leave him free.

On the ninth day while Rose was undressing me, she said to me shyly:

"It's done, Madame, from this morning."

I was a little surprised, even a touch upset, not by the thing itself, but rather by the way she told it to me. I stammered:

"And … and … it went all right?"

"Oh! Very well, Madame. For three days now he has been pestering me, but I did not want to go too fast. Madame will warn me of the moment when she wishes to catch him at it."

"Yes, my girl. Right! … Let's do it Thursday."

"It is on for Thursday, Madame. I will agree to nothing until then to keep monsieur in suspense."

"You are sure not to fail?"

"Oh! Yes, Madame, very sure. I am going to turn on monsieur for the big prize in such a fashion so as to make him give me the precise time that Madame would like best."

"Let's make it five o'clock, my good Rose."

"That's fine for five o'clock, Madame; and in what place?"

"But ….. in my bedroom."

"Very well, in Madame's bedroom."

So darling, now you understand what I did. First I went to fetch father and mother, then my uncle d'Orvelin, the president, next M. Raplet, the judge and the friend of my husband. I did not warn them what I was going to show them. I made them come in on tiptoe right up to the door of my bedroom. I waited until five o'clock precisely….. Oh! How my heart was beating. I had made the concierge come up as well to have an extra witness! And then … and then at the moment when the clock started to strike, bang, I threw the door wide open….. Ah! There it was right there ….. right there … my dear…Oh! What a face ….. what a face …if you had seen his face!…. And he turned round … the fool!

Ah! He was so funny….. I laughed, I laughed … and father, who was furious and who wanted to hit my husband….. And the concierge, a good servant, who helped him get dressed again …. in front of us … in front of us … he was buttoning his braces … what a farce!..... As for Rose she was perfect! Absolutely perfect … she was crying, she was crying very well. She is a treasure, that girl ….. if you ever need someone, don't forget her!

And here I am ….. I came straightaway to tell you about it … straightaway …I am free. Long live divorce!.....

And she started to dance in the middle of the lounge while the little baroness, thoughtful and annoyed, murmured:

Why didn't you invite me to see that?'

THE WRECK

It was yesterday, 31st December.

I had just had lunch with my old friend, George Garin. The servant brought in a letter covered with postmarks and foreign stamps.

George said to me:

"Permit me?"

"Certainly."

He started to read eight pages of large handwriting in English with crosses in every direction. He read them slowly with that serious attention and interest that one gives to subjects which touch the heart.

Then he put the letter on a corner of the mantelpiece and said:

*

Ah! There you have a curious story which I have never told you, a sentimental story though and something which happened to me! Oh! It was a peculiar New Year's day that year. That was twenty years ago …., that was when I was thirty …. And now I am fifty!

I was then a surveyor for the marine insurance company which I direct to-day. I was planning to spend the New Year in Paris, since the first of January was accepted as a holiday – when I received a letter from the director instructing me to leave immediately for the Ile de Ré where a three master from Saint-Nazaire insured by us had just been stranded. It was then eight o'clock in the morning; I arrived at the company at ten to receive the details; and the very same evening, I caught the Express which got me to La Rochelle the next day 31st December.

I had two hours before boarding the boat for Ré, the 'Jean-Guiton'[1]. I made a tour of the town. La Rochelle is really a strange city, with its streets intertwined like a labyrinth and its pavements running under endless galleries, galleries with arcades like those of the Rue de Rivoli; but they are low, these galleries and mysterious; they seemed to have been built and to exist as a stage for conspirators, as an ancient and fascinating scene for past wars, heroic and savage, the wars of religion. It is an old Huguenot city, serious and discreet, without any of those magnificent monuments which make Rouen so admirable; but it is remarkable for its totally severe appearance, also a little insidious, a city of stubborn fighters where wild schemes were planned, the town of the fanatical Calvinists – where the plot of the four sergeants[2] was hatched.

After I had wandered for some time through these peculiar streets, I boarded the black, squat little steamer which would be taking me to the Ile de Ré. It left puffing furiously and passed between the two ancient towers which guarded the port, then it crossed the channel and emerged from the sea wall built by Richelieu whose enormous boulders visible just above the water encircled the city like an immense collar. Then it veered towards the right.

It was one of those sad oppressive days, which subdued thoughts, compressed the heart and extinguished strength and energy – a grey, glacial day, drizzly and freezing, polluted by a heavy mist foul to breathe like the exhalation from a sewer.

Under this ceiling of low and sinister fog the yellow sea, shallow and sandy from the endless beaches, remained without a ripple, without a movement, lifeless, a sea of cloudy, oily and stagnant water. The 'Jean-Guiton' steamed along rolling a little as normal and slicing through this smooth, opaque slick, leaving in its wake a few slaps, a few wavelets which soon subsided.

I started to chat to the captain; he was almost bald, as round as his ship and like her rolling a little. I wanted several details on the accident which I was going to inspect. A big square rig three master from Saint-Nazaire, the 'Marie-Joseph' had gone aground in the night during a storm on the sands off the Ile de Ré.

The gale had thrown the ship so far up the sands, wrote the owner, that it had been impossible to refloat her and every thing that could be taken off,should be removed as fast as it could be unloaded. Therefore I needed to review the situation of the wreck, assess what should have been its state before the stranding, and judge if every effort had been made to refloat her. I was there as an agent of the Company to give evidence later at the proceedings, contradictory if need be.

On receiving my report, the director would take whatever steps he deemed necessary to protect our interests.

The captain knew the affair intimately since he had been called with his ship in attempts at salvage.

He told me about the disaster, very simple needless to say. The 'Marie-Joseph' driven before a strong gale, lost in the night, sailing blind on a sea of foam – "a sea of milk broth", the captain said, came to be grounded on the vast sand banks which alter the coast of this Sahara-like region during the hours of low tide.

While chatting, I was looking around me and ahead. Between the ocean and the overcast sky there was a clearance where you could see in the distance. We were following a coastline. I asked:

"Is that the Ile de Ré?"

"Yes, sir."

Then, suddenly, the captain, stretching out his right hand in front of us, pointed out to me something in the sea which was almost imperceptible and said:

"Look, there is your ship!"

"The 'Marie-Joseph'?"

"But, of course."

I was amazed. The black speck hardly visible, I would have taken it for a reef; its position appeared to me to be at least three kilometres form the coast.

I went on:

"But, captain, there must be a hundred fathoms of water at the place you have pointed out to me?"

He started to laugh.

"A hundred fathoms, my friend! …. Not two fathoms, I am telling you! ….."

He was from Bordeaux. He continued:

"It is now 0940 and we are at high water. Leave by the beach with your hands in your pockets after lunch at the Dolphin Hotel and I promise you that at 1450 or 1500 at the most, you will reach the wreck with dry feet, my friend; you will have an hour and three quarters to two hours for example to stay there, no more, before you are trapped. The further out the sea recedes, the faster it comes back. It is as flat as a pancake, this coast! Be on your way at 1650, trust me; and you will be back on board the 'Jean-Guiton' at 1930 which will see you back the same evening on the jetty at La Rochelle."

I thanked the captain and went to sit down on the foredeck of the streamer, to look at the little town of Saint-Martin which was approaching rapidly.

It resembled in miniature every harbour which serves as the capital of all the small islands scattered along the mainland coast. It was a big fishing village, one half in the water, the other on land; it lived from fish and poultry, from vegetables and scallops, from radishes and mussels. The island is very low, only a little cultivated and yet seemed very populated, but I did not penetrate the interior.

Having had lunch, I crossed a little promontory; then as the sea receded rapidly, I set off across the sands, towards a sort of black rock which I saw above the water right away in the distance.

I went swiftly over the yellow expanse, which was springy underfoot and seemed to be sweating. Only recently the sea was here and now I could only see it in the distance running out of sight and I was no longer able to distinguish the line that separated the sand from the ocean. I thought I was in the presence of some gigantic and supernatural spectacle. Just now the Atlantic was in front of me, then it had vanished into the sand like scenery through a stage trapdoor and I was walking in a desert. It was only the sensation; the tang of salt water stayed with me and I sniffed the odour of kelp and the rough and healthy smell of the waves and the seaside. I was walking fast; I was no longer cold; I was looking at the stranded wreck which was growing larger as I approached and now looked like a huge shipwrecked whale.

It appeared to be emerging from the sand and on this immense flat yellow expanse, it took on surprising proportions. I reached it at last after an hour of walking. It was lying keeled over, burst open, showing its broken bones like the ribs of a beast, bones of tarred wood pierced by enormous nails. Already the sand had invaded it, penetrating through all the cracks. It was held fast, possessed, and would no longer be set free. The bows had gone in deeply into this soft and treacherous sand while the stern raised up seemed to be appealing desperately to the sky and showed on its black planks the two words: 'Marie-Joseph'.

I scaled the hull of the ship from its lowest side; then having reached the deck, I made my way down below. Daylight showed through the sagging hatches and the fissures in the hull lit up, sadly, the long, dark holds, full of smashed woodwork. There was nothing more inside except sand which was serving as soil to the buried planks.

I started to take notes on the state of the ship. I was sitting on an empty and broken cask and I was writing by the light of a large crack through which I could see the limitless extent of the shore. From time to time a peculiar shiver of cold and solitude ran down my skin; occasionally I stopped writing to listen to the strange and mysterious noises of the wreck; the noise of crabs scratching at the planking with their hooked claws, the noise of a thousand little sea creatures already settled on the corpse, and also the quiet, regular noise of the barnacles, which continued to gnaw and bore into the old timbers, digging and devouring them.

Suddenly I heard the sound of human voices quite close to me. I jumped up as if I had seen a ghost. For a second I really thought that I was going to see emerging from that sinister hold two of the drowned crew who would relate the circumstances of their death. To be sure, using the strength of my wrists, it did not take me long to clamber up on to the deck and standing up, I saw in front of the vessel a large gentleman with three young girls, or, rather a large Englishman with three young misses. Certainly they were much more frightened than me when they saw this being rapidly appearing from the abandoned three master. The youngest girl ran off; the two others grabbed their father with both arms and as for him, his mouth dropped open and that was the only sign which betrayed his emotion.

Then after a few seconds, he spoke:

"What ho, sir, are you the proprietor of this ship?"

"Yes, sir."

"Could I visit it?"

"Yes, sir"

Then he uttered a long sentence in English of which I could only make out one word – 'gracious' – repeated several times.

As he was looking for a place to climb up, I showed him the best spot and lent him a hand. He made it up and then we helped the three girls who were now reassured. They were charming, especially the eldest, a blond eighteen year old, fresh as a flower, so graceful, so cute! Pretty English girls really do seem like tender fruit of the sea. One would have said that the eldest had just come out of the sand and that her hair had retained the shade. With their exquisite freshness, they all made one think of the delicate colours of pink shells, of mother of pearl, rare and mysterious and hatched in the uncharted depths of the ocean.

The eldest spoke French a little better than her father and she acted as our interpreter. I had to recount the story of the shipwreck in the smallest details which I made up as if I had been present at the disaster. Then the whole family descended into the interior of the wreck. As soon as they had entered that dark gallery which had hardly any light, they uttered cries of astonishment and wonder; then, immediately, the father and his three daughters produced sketch pads, doubtless concealed in their large waterproof coats and all four at the same time started four pencil sketches of the strange gloomy scene.

They were seated side by side on a projecting beam and the four sketch pads on four pairs of knees were covered with small black lines to represent the half open hold of the 'Marie-Joseph'.

Working all the time, the eldest of the girls chatted to me while I continued to inspect the skeleton of the vessel.

I learned that they were spending the winter in Biarritz and they had come to the Ile de Ré expressly to see the stranded three master. They had none of the English arrogance these people. They were the simple, nice, slightly crazy type of eternal wanderer which England spreads across the globe. The father was tall, reserved, his red face framed by white side whiskers, a real living sandwich, a leg of ham cut as a human head between two tufts of hair; the girls long legged like little young herons were also all except the eldest, reserved; all three were nice especially the tallest.

She had a funny way of speaking, of describing, of laughing, of understanding and not understanding, of raising her deep blue eyes to ask me a question, a funny way of saying 'yes' or 'no', a funny way of stopping and restarting her drawing, a funny way of guessing what to say next. I could have watched her and listened to her indefinitely.

Suddenly she murmured:

"I heard a slight movement of this vessel."

I pricked up my ears, and straightaway I made out a small, peculiar continuous noise. What was it? I got up to go and look through the crack, and let out a violent exclamation. The sea had rejoined us and was going to surround us!

We were on the deck immediately. It was too late. The water was all round us and was running towards the coast at a prodigious speed. No, not exactly running, it was creeping, sliding, spreading like an enormous stain. Although there was hardly a few centimetres covering the sand, already we could no longer see the fleeing line which marked the imperceptible movement of the tide.

The Englishman was all for jumping off; I held him back. Flight was impossible on account of the deep water we had to skirt round when we arrived and into which we would stumble on our return.

In our hearts there was a minute of horrible anguish. Then the little English girl started to smile and murmured:

"Now it is us who are shipwrecked!"

I wanted to laugh; but fear restrained me, fear which was cowardly and awful, low and insidious like the tide. All the dangers that we would meet occurred to me at the same time. I wanted to shout: "Help!" But to whom?

The two small girls were huddled against their father who was looking with consternation at the sea spreading round us.

And as quickly as the ocean rose, night was falling. a dark, damp and icy night.

I said:

"There is nothing for it except to stay on the ship."

The Englishman replied:

"Oh! Yes!"

We stayed there for an quarter of an hour, half an hour, truly, I did not know how long it was – watching that yellow water, deepening, turning and seemingly boiling around us and which appeared to be gambolling on that immense recaptured shore.

One of the small girls was cold and we had the idea to go back down below to shelter from the light but icy wind which was blowing over us and prickling our skin.

I leant over the hatch. The vessel was full of water. So we had to huddle against the bulwarks at the stern which gave us a little protection.

Darkness was now enveloping us and we stayed squeezed one against another surrounded by water and gloom. Against my shoulder, I felt the shoulder of the eldest girl trembling and, at times, her teeth were chattering; but I also felt the soft warmth of her body through the material of her clothing and that warmth was delicious like a kiss. We were not talking any more; we remained motionless, dumb, crouched like animals in a ditch during the hours of a storm. Yet despite everything, despite the night, despite the terrible and growing danger, I started to feel happy to be there, happy with the cold and the peril, happy to spend long, dark and anxious hours on these planks of wood so close to this pretty and cute girl.

I wondered why this curious feeling of well-being and joy was getting to me.

Why? Do we know? Because she was there? Why her? A little English girl, a complete stranger. I did not love her, I did not even know her and I felt moved, conquered! I would have wanted to save her, to have devoted myself to her, to have done a thousand foolish things for her? Odd thing! How is it that the presence of a woman can bowl us over like that? Is it the power of her charm which enraptures us? The seduction of her youth and beauty which intoxicates us like wine?

Is it not rather the sort of attraction which love has, the mysterious love which seeks continually to unite people, which puts its power to the test as soon as a man and a woman are facing one another and fills them with emotion, a secret, deep, and confused emotion, like when the earth is soaked to push up the flowers!

The silence of the sky and the darkness, however, was becoming frightening, because we were vaguely hearing all around us a gentle, continuous rustling sound, the murmur of the silent sea which was rising and the monotonous slaps of the tide against the hull.

Suddenly I heard sobs. The youngest little girl was crying, so her father wanted to console her and they started to speak in their language which I did not understand. I guessed that he was reassuring her and that she was still frightened.

I asked my neighbour:

"Miss, are you sure that you are not too cold?"

"Oh, yes, I am very cold."

I wanted to give her my jacket, but she refused it; but I had already taken it off and, in spite of her, I put it round her shoulders. In the short struggle I encountered her hand which gave me a delicious thrill all over.

For several minutes now the air had become sharper and the slapping of the waves against the sides of the vessel louder. I stood up; a big gust hit my face. The wind was getting up!

The Englishman had seen it the same time as me and said simply:

"It is bad for us this ....."

Definitely it was bad; it was certain death if the breakers, even small breakers arrived to attack and buffet the wreck, which was so smashed and dislocated that the first slightly severe wave would carry it away in pieces.

So our anxiety grew from second to second with the gusts growing stronger and stronger. Now the waves were breaking a little and in the darkness I was seeing dark lines of foam appearing and disappearing, while each surge crashed against the carcass of the 'Marie-Joseph', shaking it with a brief shudder which went right to our hearts.

The girl was trembling. I felt her shivering against me and I had a mad urge to clasp her in my arms.

In the distance to the left, to the right and behind us, the lighthouses on the coast beamed, revolving, white, yellow and red like enormous eyes, gigantic eyes looking at us, watching us, waiting avidly for us to disappear. One of them in particular irritated me. It flashed and went out every thirty seconds. It really was an eye that one with its eyelid regularly lowered over its fiery eyeball.

Occasionally the Englishman struck a match to look at the time; then he put his watch back in his pocket. Suddenly over the heads of his daughters he said with supreme seriousness:

"Monsieur, I wish you a happy New Year."

It was midnight. We shook hands; then he pronounced some words in English and suddenly he and his daughters started to sing 'God Save the Queen' which floated upwards into the black and speechless air and evaporated into space ....

At first I wanted to laugh; then I was seized with a strange and powerful emotion.

There was something sinister and magnificent about this song from a condemned and shipwrecked crew like a prayer and also something greater, comparable to the ancient and sublime, 'Ave Caesar, morituri te salutant'[(3)].

When they had finished, I asked my neighbour to sing a ballad solo, a tale whatever she liked to make us forget our anxiety. She consented and immediately her clear and young voice took off into the night. Without a doubt she sang something sad for the notes, leaving her mouth slowly trailed for a long time, fluttering above the waves like wounded birds.

The seas got bigger and were now battering the wreck. Personally I was no longer thinking of anything except this voice, and I was thinking also of sirens; if a ship had passed close to us, what would the sailors had said? My tormented mind was lost in a dream! A siren! Was she not in fact a siren, this girl of the sea who was keeping me on this worm eaten vessel and who presently would plunge with me into the waves? …..

But suddenly all five of us were rolling along the deck, for the 'Marie-Joseph' had subsided on to her starboard side. The girl had fallen on top of me; I clasped her in my arms and madly, without realising it, without knowing what I was doing, believing that my last moment had come, I kissed her fully on the cheek, on the forehead and on the hair. The boat did not shift any more; also the rest of us were not moving.

Her father said: "Kate!" As I was holding her, she replied: "Yes" and made a movement to disengage herself. Certainly at that moment I would have wished that the boat had split in two so I could have fall into the water with her.

He went on:

"A little upset, it was nothing. I have my three girls safe."

Not having seen the eldest, at first he had believed her lost!

Slowly I got up and suddenly I saw a light on the water quite close to us. I shouted; they replied. It was a boat looking for us; the proprietor of the hotel had foreseen our imprudence.

We were saved. I was sorry! They plucked us from our raft and took us to Saint-Martin.

Now the Englishman was rubbing his hands and muttering: "Now for a good supper! A good supper!"

In fact we had supper but I was not cheerful. I regretted the 'Marie-Joseph'.

It was necessary to part the next day and after many hugs and promises to write they left for Biarritz. There was little need for me to follow them.

I was bowled over. I had nearly proposed to that girl. Certainly if we had spent eight days together I would have married her! How very often is the man sometimes weak and incomprehensible!

Two years went by without receiving any news from them; then I had a letter from New York. She told me she was married and since then we have exchanged letters every year on the 1st January. She told me about her life, spoke about her children and her sisters – never her husband! Why? Ah! Why? ….. And me, I only spoke to her of the 'Marie-Joseph' ….. She was the only woman perhaps whom I might have loved ……… whom I would have loved ….. Ah! ….. look ….. do we know? ….. We get carried away by events ….. and then …..everything passes. Now she must be old ….. I would not recognise her …. Ah! The girl from the past ….. the girl from the wreck ….. what a divine creature! She writes to say that her hair is now quite white ….. My God ….. that upsets me horribly ….. Ah! that blond hair ….. No, mine no longer exists ….. How sad ….. all that! …..

A NEW YEAR'S PRESENT

Jacques de Randal, having dined alone at home, told his servant that he could leave; then he sat down at his table to write some letters.

He ended every year like this alone, writing and daydreaming. For his own benefit he produced a sort of review of past events since the last day of the previous year, events concluded, things over and done with; and as the faces of his friends rose up in front of his eyes, he wrote them a few lines, a cordial greeting for 1st of January.

So he sat down, opened a drawer and from inside took out a photograph of a woman, he looked at it for a few seconds and kissed it. Than having put it down beside his sheet of paper, he began:

"My dear Irène, you should shortly receive the little reminder that I address to the woman I love. I have shut myself in this evening to tell you....."

His pen remained motionless. Jaques got up and started to pace up and down.

He had had a mistress for ten months, not a mistress on the make, from society, the theatre or the street, but a woman he had loved and conquered. He was no longer a young man although still young in outlook and he regarded life seriously in a positive and pragmatic spirit.

Therefore he began to set out the assessment of his passion as he used to do every year, also the balance sheet of friendships, new or disappeared, the events and the people who had come into his life.

His first burning love had calmed down; he wondered with the precision of a tradesman doing his accounts what was the state of his heart for her now and he tried to work out what it would be in the future.

He found there a great and deep affection, resulting from love, appreciation, and the thousand minute ties from which long and strong liaisons are born.

The sound of his bell made him start. He hesitated. Should he open the door? But he said to himself that one should always open on New Year's Eve, open to a stranger who was passing and knocking on the door – whoever he might be.

So he took a candle, crossed the hall, pulled back the bolts, turned the key and opened the door; he saw his mistress standing there, pale as a death, leaning against the wall with her hands.

He stammered:

"What is the matter?"

She replied:

"Are you alone?"

"Yes."

"Without servants?"

"Yes."

"You are not going out?"

"No."

She came in like a woman who knew the house. As soon as she was in the drawing room, she slumped down on the couch, covered her face with her hands and began to weep dreadfully.

He knelt down in front of her and forcing her arms open to see her eyes, he repeated:

"Irène, Irène, what is it? I implore you, tell me what is the matter?"

Then in the middle of her sobbing, she murmured:

"I cannot go on living like this."

He didn't understand.

"Live like this? … How…..?"

"Yes, I cannot go on living like this ….. at home… You have no idea ….. I have never told you ….. I am suffering too much….. He has often slapped me….."

"Who….. Your husband?"

"Yes… My husband."

"Ah! …"

He was astonished, having never suspected that her husband could be brutal. He was a figure in society, the best, a club man, a horseman, a swordsman, influential behind the scenes; well known quoted and appreciated everywhere, he had very courteous manners, although a very average mind; the lack of education and intelligence is essential in order to think like well brought up people and to have a proper respect for every prejudice.

He seemed to treat his wife as one should amongst rich and well born types. He took sufficient trouble as regards her clothes, her health and her wishes, and, besides, allowed her total freedom.

Randal had become friendly with Irène and had the right to an affectionate handshake which every husband who knows how to behave, owes to the regular friends of his wife. Then when Jacques, having been for some time the friend, became the lover, his relation with the husband became more cordial as if it was accepted.

He had never seen nor guessed the storms in that house, and in the face of this unexpected revelation, he continued to be alarmed.

He asked:

"Tell me how did it happen?"

Then she recounted a long story, the whole history of her life from the day of her marriage. The first dissension arose from a nothing, then became more marked as a result of every difference which increased each day between two opposite characters.

Next came quarrels and complete separation which although not apparent, in actual fact existed; then her husband became surly, aggressive and violent. Now he was jealous, jealous of Jacques and that very day, after a scene, he had slapped her.

She added with firmness: "I will no longer return home to him. Do with me what you will."

Jacques was sitting face to face with her; their knees were touching. He took her hands:

"My dear friend, you are going to commit a gross and irreparable stupidity. If you wish to leave your husband, put him in the wrong in such a way that your situation as the wife, the wife of irreproachable social position, remains secure."

Throwing him an anxious glance, she asked:

"Then, what do you advise?"

"Return home and put up with the life until the day when you will be able to obtain maybe a separation, maybe a divorce[1], with full military honours."

"Is that not a little cowardly, what you are advising there?"

"No, it is wise and reasonable. You have a high social position, a name to safeguard, friends to keep, parents to handle. You must not forget it and lose all that through a sudden rush of blood to the head."

She rose violently: "Oh! No, I cannot any longer, it is finished, it is finished, it is finished!"

Then putting her hands on the shoulders of her lover and looking at him straight in the eye:

"Do you love me?"

"Yes."

"Truthfully?"

"Yes."

"Then, keep me."

He cried out:

"Keep you? With me? Here? But you are crazy! That would lose you everything for ever; you will be lost without any comeback! You are mad!"

She replied slowly and gravely like a woman who feels the weight of her words.

"Listen, Jacques. He has forbidden me to see you again and I will not play the comedy of coming to you in secret. You must lose me or take me."

"My dear Irène, in that case obtain your divorce and I will marry you."

"Yes, you will marry me in ….. two years at the earliest. You have a lasting affection."

"Look, think about it. If you stay here, he will take you back tomorrow, since he is your husband, since he has the right and the law on his side."

"I was not asking you, Jacques, to keep me at your house but to take me away, no matter where. I believed that you loved me enough for that. I was wrong. Goodbye."

She turned round and made for the door so quickly that he only managed to grab her when she had gone out of the lounge.

"Listen, Irène…."

She put up a struggle not wishing to hear any more; with her eyes full of tears, she stammered: "Let me go ….. let me go … let me go."

He forced her to sit down and again went on his knees in front of her, then, piling up reasons and advice, he tried to make her understand the folly and frightful danger of her project. He did not forget anything he needed to say to convince her, looking for motives even in his affection for his conviction.

Since she remained icily silent, he begged her, he implored her to listen to him, to believe him and to follow his advice.

When he had finished speaking, she simply replied:

"Are you disposed to let me leave now? Release me so I can get up."

"Look, Irène…."

"Will you let me go?"

"Irène ….. your resolve is irrevocable?"

"Will you release me!"

"Simply tell me if your resolve, if your mad resolve which you will bitterly regret is irrevocable?"

"Yes ….. let me go."

"Then, stay. You know very well that you are at your home here. We will leave tomorrow morning."

She got up in spite of him and said harshly:

"No, it is too late. I do not want sacrifice, I do not want devotion."

"Stay. I have done what I ought to have done. I have said what I had to say. Regarding you I am no longer responsible. My conscience is clear. Express your wishes and I will obey."

She sat down again, looked at him for a long time, then in a very calm voice she asked:

"Then, explain."

"What? What do you want me to explain?"

"Everything….. Everything you have thought of to change my resolve just like that. Then I, personally, will see what I must do."

"But I have not thought of anything at all. I had to warn you that you were going to act foolishly. You persist, I am asking for my part in this folly and I even require it."

"It is not natural to change an opinion so quickly."

"Listen, my dear friend. In this case it is neither a question of sacrifice nor devotion. The day when I realised that I loved you, I told myself what every person in love should say in the same situation, that is:

"The man who loves a woman, who tries hard to conquer her, who gets her and takes her, contracts with himself and with her a sacred obligation. Of course it is a question of a woman like you, not a woman with an accessible and easy heart.

Marriage which has a huge social value and a huge legal value in my opinion has only a very small moral value, given the conditions in which it usually takes place.

Therefore when a woman, tied by the legal bond but who does not love her husband, who cannot love him and whose heart is free, meets a man who pleases her and gives herself to him and when a man without ties takes a woman in the same way, I am telling you that they are obligated vis-à-vis one another through that free and mutual consent much more than through the 'yes' murmured in front of the mayor's sash.

I am telling you that if they are both totally honourable people, their union has to be more intimate, stronger and healthier than all the sacraments of marriage.

That woman risks everything. And it is precisely because she knows it that she gives everything, her heart, her body, her soul, her honour, her life; because she has foreseen all the misery, all the dangers and disasters, because she risks a bold and fearless act, because she is ready and determined to face up to every-thing – a husband who could kill her, and society who could reject her – it is for that reason that she is honest in her conjugal infidelity – that is why her lover in taking her must also have foreseen everything and must prefer her to everything whatever may happen. At first I spoke as a sensible person who should have warned you, now there is nothing more for me than to be a man, the man who loves you. Decide."

Radiant she silenced his mouth with her lips and said in a whisper:

"It wasn't true, darling. There was no problem. My husband suspects nothing. But I wanted to see, I wanted to know what you would do, I wanted some present ……. One from your heart and a different New Year's present from the occasional neck-lace. You have given it to me. Thank you …..thanks ….God, I am happy!"

THE TRAVELLING SALESMAN

There are often brief memories of small incidents, encounters, modest dramas which for our still young and ignorant minds are like threads leading little by little to the knowledge of the depressing truth.

Every time I pause and reflect during periods when my thoughts are wandering, thoughts which distract me on roads where I am haphazardly strolling, during flights of fancy I suddenly rediscover small facts in the past, either cheerful or sinister, which take off in front of my daydream like birds which fly out of the bushes in front of me.

This summer I was wandering along a country road in Savoie from which there was a view of the shore of lake Bourget; I was gazing at that expanse of shimmering blue water, a unique pale blue, dappled with the slanting rays of the declining sun and I felt stirring in my heart that attachment which I have had since childhood for the surfaces of lakes, rivers and the sea. On the other edge of that huge watery plain, so extended that its extremities – one falling towards the Rhone, the other to Bourget – a high mountain rose up with jagged crests the last one being the point of the Dent-au-Chat. On the other side of the road rows of vines ran from tree to tree smothering under their foliage the frail branches with their supports; across the fields they developed into chains, green, yellow and red garlands, festooned from one stem to another and conspicuous with bunches of black grapes.

The road was deserted, powdery and white. Suddenly a man emerged from a grove of large trees which enclosed the village of Saint-Innocent, and bending down under the weight of a burden, he came towards me leaning on a stick.

When he was closer, I recognised that he was a pedlar, one of those travelling salesmen who sells small items at bargain prices from door to door in country districts and that reminded me of a very old story, practically nothing, of an encounter I had one night between Argenteuil and Paris when I was twenty-five.

At this time, all the joy in my life consisted in sculling. I had a room from the owner of a café at Argenteuil, and each evening I caught the bureaucrats' train, that long slow train which dropped from station to station a crowd of men in small packets, men who were ungainly and paunchy because, with their baggy trousers so worn out by office chairs, they could scarcely walk. This train in which I reckoned to find again the smell of the office, the green boxes and the files of papers, dropped me at Argenteuil. My skiff was waiting for me there, ready to go on to the water. With the long strokes of my oars I used to row to my dinner, maybe at Bezon, maybe Chatou, possibly at Epinay or Saint-Ouen. Then I used to return, put my boat away and set off back to Paris when the moon was overhead.

But then, one night on that bare road, I saw a man walking in front of me; Oh! Nearly every time I would run into these night travellers in the Paris suburbs who were so much feared by the bourgeoisie who were out late. This man was going along slowly in front of me weighed down by a heavy pack.

I came right up to him at a fast pace and my footsteps were resounding on the road. He stopped and turned round and then, as I was still approaching him, he crossed the roadway, and reached the other side.

Then, after I had swiftly passed him, he shouted at me:

"Hi, evening, sir."

I replied:

"Evening, mate."

He responded:

"Are you going far this way?"

"I am going to Paris."

"You will not take long. You are walking fast. Me, I have my pack too loaded up to go quickly."

I slowed my pace.

Why was this man speaking to me? What was he transporting in that big pack? Vague suspicions of some crime crossed my mind and made me curious. Various details were reported each morning in the newspapers of acts carried out at this very place, the Gennevilliers peninsular, and some of them must have been true. All those whole columns entrusted to reporters, containing the full litany of arrests and various misdemeanours, not all of them are invented just to please readers.

Yet the voice of this man seemed rather more timid than bold and his attitude up till then more careful than aggressive.

I asked him in my turn:

"You, are you going far?"

"No further than Asnières."

"Is it your district, Asnières?"

"Yes, sir, I am a travelling salesman by profession and I live in Asnières."

He had left the sidewalk in the shade of the trees used by pedestrians during the day and he approached the middle of the road. I did the same thing. We were looking at each other the whole time with a suspicious eye holding our sticks in our hands. When I was near enough next to him, I was quite re-assured. Certainly he was as well because he asked me:

"Would it matter to you at all if you went a little less fast?"

"Why do you ask?"

"Because I don't like this road here in the night. I have merchandise on my back; it is always better to be two rather than one. They do not often attack two men when they are together."

I sensed that he was telling the truth and that he was afraid. So I fell in with his wishes, and there we were, walking side by side, this stranger and me, at one o'clock in the morning on the road which led from Argenteuil to Asnières.

"How is it that you are returning so late and running a risk?" I asked my neighbour.

He told me his story.

154

He had not thought of returning this evening, having taken away with him that same morning enough merchandise for three or four days.

But sales had been very good, so good that he was obliged to return home immediately in order to deliver tomorrow many things which had been purchased on trust.

He explained with real satisfaction that he used to give the sales pitch very well having a particular aptitude in that respect, and what he could demonstrate with his samples especially helped him, while chatting, to sell those things he could not easily carry with him.

He added:

"I have a shop at Asnières. It is my wife who runs it."

"Ah! You are married?"

"Yes, sir, fifteen month ago. I have found a nice woman. She is going to be surprised to see me coming back home to-night."

He told me about his marriage. He had courted this girl for two years but she had taken time to make up her mind.

She had kept a little shop on a street corner since childhood where she sold everything; ribbons, flowers in the summer, very pretty boot buckles and several other ornaments in which she specialised thanks to a manufacturer. In Asnières she was well known and was called La Bluette because she often wore blue dresses. Also she earned money and was extremely adroit at everything she did. Just now she seemed to be ill. He thought she was pregnant but he could not be sure. Their business was going well; above all he travelled – to show samples to all the small trades people in the neighbouring localities; he had become a sort of travelling rep for certain firms and he worked at the same time both for them and for himself.

"And you, what do you do?" he said.

I was embarrassed. I told him that at Argenteuil I owned a sailing boat and two racing skiffs. I came to practise sculling every evening, and, liking the exercise, sometimes I went back to Paris where I had a profession which I let him guess was lucrative.

He answered:

"Christ, I wish I had fun and games like you. As for me I do not enjoy exposing myself on these roads like this in the night. It is not safe round here."

He gave me a sidelong look and I wondered if he was not, all the same, a very clever criminal who did not want to run a pointless risk.

Then he reassured me, murmuring:

"Not so fast, please, my pack is heavy."

The first houses in Asnières appeared.

"I see that we are nearly there," he said, "we don't sleep at the shop; it is guarded at night by a dog, but a dog which is worth four men. And then housing is too dear in the centre of the town. But, listen, sir, you have rendered me a great service, for my heart is not easy on the roads with my bag. And, well, by rights, you will come home to drink a punch with my wife, if she is awake, because she sleeps very soundly and does not like it when she is roused. After that I will escort you to the entrance of the town with my cudgel. Without my pack, I have nothing to fear."

I refused, he insisted, I was obstinate. He persevered with such trouble, with such sincere desperation, with such phrases of regret – for he did not express himself badly – asking me with a wounded look as 'if it was that I did not wish to drink with the likes of him' that I ended up giving in; so I followed him down a deserted track towards one of those big dilapidated houses in a suburban quarter.

In front of this dwelling, I hesitated. That tall plaster building had the air of a den for squatters, of a barracks for down town villains; but after pushing open the door, which was not locked, he made me go on ahead. He piloted me by the shoulders in the pitch darkness towards the stairs where I was groping with my feet and hands in the justifiable fear of falling into a hole or a cellar.

When I bumped into the first step, he told me: "Keep on going up, it is on the sixth."

156

Searching my pockets, I discovered a box of match-lights and I lit up the ascent. He was following me, puffing with his bag repeating: "It is high! It is high!"

When we reached the top of the house, he searched for his key which was attached to a string inside his clothes, then he opened the door and got me to go inside.

It was a whitewashed room with a table in the middle, six chairs and a kitchen cupboard against the wall.

"I am going to wake up my wife, " he said, "then I will go down to the cellar to fetch some wine; it is not kept here."

He went to one of the doors leading off from this first room and called out: "Bluette! Bluette!" Bluette did not respond. Then knocking on the woodwork with his fist, he muttered: "In God's name, will you wake up!"

He waited, stuck his ear against the keyhole and said calmly: "Bah! We'll have to let her sleep if she is sleeping. I'll go and fetch the wine, expect me back in a couple of minutes."

He went out and resignedly I sat down.

What on earth was I doing there? Suddenly I started. For someone was whispering, gently stirring almost noiselessly in the woman's bedroom.

Devil! Had I not fallen into a trap? Why had she not woken up, this Bluette, with all the noise her husband had made, with the blows with which he had knocked on the door? Was it a signal to tell accomplices: "There is a victim in the bag. I am going to guard the exit. Over to you." For sure someone was moving more and more; they were trying the lock and turning the key. My heart was beating. I withdrew to the back of the apartment saying to myself: "Come on, defend yourself!" and grabbing a wooden chair by its back with both hands, I got ready for a violent struggle.

The door was ajar and a hand now held it half open, then a head, a head of a man with a round felt cap slipped between the door panel and the wall; I saw two eyes looking at me. Then so quickly that I did not have time to make a defensive movement, the presumed criminal, a big lad, hastily dressed without a tie, slippers in his hands, a handsome lad, my God, almost a gentleman, bounded for the exit and disappeared down the stairs.

I sat down again, the adventure was becoming amusing. Then I waited for the husband who was a long time finding his wine. At last I heard him climbing the stairs and the noise of his footsteps made me laugh, one of those solitary laughs which are so hard to stifle.

He came in carrying two bottles, then he asked me:

"My wife is still asleep. You haven't heard her stirring?"

I imagined the ear stuck against the door and I said:

"No, not at all."

He called out again:

"Pauline!"

She did not reply nor did she stir. He came back to me, explaining:

"You see, what she doesn't like is when I come back in the night to have a drink with a friend."

"Then you reckon that she is not asleep?"

"For sure, she is no longer asleep."

He had a disgruntled look.

"Ah well! Let's have a drink," he said.

And he manifested the intention of emptying the two bottles, there and then, one after the other, quite slowly.

This time I was firm. I drank a glass, then I rose. He no longer spoke of escorting me; he was looking at his wife's door with a hard stare, the look of a man of the people who was angry, the look of a brute in whom violence was sleeping and he muttered:

"She really will have to open up after you have left."

I summed him up, this coward who had become furious without knowing why, perhaps having the dark suspicion, the instinct of the deceived male who does not like doors to be locked. He had spoken to me about her with affection; now for sure he was going to give her a beating.

He shouted once again, shaking the door handle:

"Pauline!"

A voice, which seemed to be awake, replied from behind the partition:

"Sorry, what is it?"

"Didn't you hear me coming in?"

"No, I was asleep, leave me in peace."

"Open your door."

"When you are alone. I don't like it when you bring back men to drink in the house at night."

Then I went away, stumbling on the stairs, like the other one who had departed and whose accomplice I had been. And getting back on the road for Paris, I was reflecting on what I had just witnessed in that slum, a scene of the eternal drama which is played every day, in every form, in every society.

NOTES

All the stories in this book (except the last one) originally appeared in newspapers and were then included in various collections which Maupassant arranged with his publishers. These collections usually featured one of the longer stories as the title. One of the newspapers which Maupassant particularly favoured was the *"Gil Blas'* a popular and light hearted journal and of the nineteen stories translated in this bookonly four (which have been noted) did not appear in the *'Gil Blas'* . The following is the list of the stories with their French titles, the year in which they first appeared and the titles of the books in which they were later published. The translations have been made from the folio classique series of Maupassant published in recent years by Gallimard.

The Rondoli Sisters (*Les Soeurs Rondoli*) 1884 Echo de Paris reprinted in Les Soeurs Rondoli.
A Parisian adventure (*Une aventure Parisienne*) 1881 reprinted in Mademoiselle Fifi.
The Log (*La Bûche*) 1882 Le Gaulois reprinted in Mademoiselle Fifi.
Moonlight (*Clair de Lune*) 1882 reprinted in Le Père Milon.
A Passion (*Une Passion*) 1882 reprinted in Le Père Milon.
At The Bedside (*Au bord du Lit*) 1883 reprinted in Monsieur Parent.
Goodbye (*Adieu*) 1884 reprinted in Contes du Jour et de la Nuit.
The Landlady (*La Patronne*) 1884 reprinted in Les Soeurs Rondoli.

A Memory (*Souvenir*) 1884 reprinted in Contes du Jour et de la Nuit.

Father Boniface's Crime (*La Crime de Père Boniface*) 1884 reprinted in Contes du Jour et de la Nuit.

Bombard (*Bombard*) 1884 reprinted in Toine.

The Room 11 (*la Chambre 11*) 1884 reprinted in Toine.

The Cupboard (*L'Armoire*) 1884 reprinted in Toine.

Roger's Method (*Le Moyen de Roger*) 1885 reprinted in Toine.'

A Failure (*Un Échec*) 1885 reprinted in Le Rosier de Madame Husson

Saved (*Sauvée*) 1885 reprinted in La Petite Roque.

The Wreck (*L'Épave*) 1886 Le Gaulois reprinted in La Petite Roque.

A New Year's Present (*Etrennes*) 1887 reprinted in Le Père Milon.

The Travelling Salesman (*Le Colporteur*) There is no record of this story having been published in a newspaper but it was included in the collection – Le Père Milon published 1899 six years after Maupassant's death.

Many of these stories mention the names of individuals known to Maupassant and the following notes provide more details as well as explaining some of the more obscure references:

The Rondoli Sisters

(1) 'A Poet' – Louis Bouhilet (1822-69) a friend of Flaubert (1821-80).

(2) "Non capisco" – "I do not understand."

(3) "Che mi fa" – "What's that to do with me."

(4) "Mica" – "Not at all."

(5) *'To conquer without danger, is to triumph without glory'* – An often quoted French maxim from El Cid by Corneille (1606-84).

(6) 'Titian's famous lady' – The very well known painting 'Venus at Rest'.

A Parisian Adventure

(1) 'Monsieur Busnach' (1832-1907) – A recognised playwright who adapted the novels of Zola for the theatre.

(2) 'Alexander Dumas' (1824-1895) – A dramatist and son of the famous novelist.

(3) Monsieur Zola – Emile Zola (1840-1902) – Another famous novelist.

Moonlight

(1) 'Musset' – Alfred de Musset (1810-1867) – A very well known French poet and dramatist.

Goodbye

(1) 'The war' – Franco – Prussian war 1870.

Bombard

(1) 'King Midas barber' – Midas was the mythical king of Phrygia who turned to gold anything he touched. This reference is to another fable about Midas; Apollo gave him ass's ears which he concealed under his cap; only his barber knew the secret and was forbidden to reveal it but the barber told the reeds by the river who whispered it to the wind.

The Cupboard

(1) 'Follies-Bergère' – The establishment was built in 1869.

Roger's Method

(1) 'Sire of Brantome' – A French knight from the Middle Ages who wrote memoirs about ladies alluding to Roger's problem.

A Failure

(1) 'Echo of Paris' – A journal founded in 1884 was a competitor to the 'Gil Blas'. Aurelien Scholl was the editor.

(2) 'Felix Frank' – A little known poet whom Maupassant may have thought needed some publicity.